T0245703

adam

ADVANCE PRAISE FOR THE BOOK

'S. Hareesh, in these astonishing stories, takes an honest joy in human villainy and reveals a painful and comical truth—exuberant violence, determined greed and pure spite are the stuff of our relations with each other, with animals and with the world at large'—Anjum Hasan, author

'An inspired translation of a brilliant constellation of stories, rooted in language and landscape, within a narrative arc that is vast and universal. S. Hareesh's imagination evades the limitations of Anthropocene consciousness to give us a master class in the craft of storytelling'—Namita Gokhale, author, and director, Jaipur Literature Festival

'Hareesh's writing carries, always, the unexpected, the uncanny. In this collection of short fiction, we encounter worlds within worlds, stories within stories—a gloriously tangled web of lives that intersect in hilariously unsavoury, yet always human, ways. From dogs and their "masters", old lifelong enemies who can't, quite literally, live without each other, a traveller who walks down a road on an endless night, men with magic tails, bulls that break free, we are borne away by a telling that's informed by the wild, the oral, the unruly. Through this, Hareesh dissects for us, in scathing, often laugh-out-loud ways, the facades adopted by masculinity, civility, caste. In these stories, humans are human in such achingly real ways that what's also conjured is the unbelievable, the farcical, the beasts'—Janice Pariat, author

adam

S. HAREESH

Translated from the Malayalam by

Jayasree Kalathil

VINTAGE

An imprint of Penguin Random House

VINTAGE

USA | Canada | UK | Ireland | Australia
New Zealand | India | South Africa | China

Vintage is part of the Penguin Random House group of companies
whose addresses can be found at global.penguinrandomhouse.com

Published by Penguin Random House India Pvt. Ltd
4th Floor, Capital Tower 1, MG Road,
Gurugram 122 002, Haryana, India

This edition published in Vintage by Penguin Random House India Private Ltd
by arrangement with DC Books

10 9 8 7 6 5 4 3 2

ISBN 9780670094608

Typeset in Sabon by Manipal Technologies Limited, Manipal
Printed at Thomson Press India Ltd, New Delhi

www.penguin.co.in

Contents

Foreword

Readers of my work in English would only be familiar with *Moustache*. Before writing the novel, I published three collections of short stories in Malayalam. *Adam* is the second of those.

The collection has a special place in my heart for several reasons. After my first book came out, I had to stay away from writing for a number of years—years when I thought I might never write again. The stories in this collection helped me come out of that state of mind. They also mark a turning point for the writer that I am today in terms of my writing style, language and choice of subjects.

The nine stories in this collection reflect the language and lifestyle of the land where I was born and grew up. I am of the opinion that our writing is affected by the people we meet and the books we read. In that sense, this collection owes a debt of gratitude to those around me and the stories I have read so far.

I am very pleased that Jayasree Kalathil, my dear friend and the translator of *Moustache*, has translated these stories too. Jayasree's excellence in her craft needs no reiteration from me. Readers of literature translated into English have ample evidence in front of them.

Adam was read quite widely in Malayalam, going into ten reprints and receiving the Kerala Sahitya Akademi Award for short story in 2016. I am grateful to Penguin Random House and editor Elizabeth Kuruvilla for their enthusiasm about the book and the opportunity to bring it to a wider audience. I can only hope that it will be received well and read widely.

Neendoor S. Hareesh

adam

On 26 December 1970, ex-serviceman N.K. Kuruppu rushed home with a puppy of a special breed. It was evident from the speed of the car in which he was travelling that he was impatient to meet his son, born the night before after procrastinating for many years. Kuruppu had always been an impatient man, even when he was in the army. When he would come home on leave, young men loitering at the junction would watch his taxi zip down the road from the train station and, thinking of his wife waiting for him, exclaim: 'Look at him go! He has already removed his underpants and slung them over his shoulder!'

A sense of lethargy now pervaded the junction, still recovering from the festivities of Christmas. The chai shop and the barber shop were closed. Two middle-aged men and a few young men stood in front of one of the two paan shops which was open. One of the young men was feeling pleased with himself for having engraved the words 'May a thousand flowers bloom' on the back wall of the public urinal, a feat he had accomplished after several months of careful planning.

All of them caught a glimpse of the puppy's head as the car sped past them. Still, unwilling to trust their own eyes, they followed the car, walking briskly down the road. The Kuruppu they knew was not the type to love a human child, let alone the child of a dog. He was the type of soldier who was feared and respected even by his enemies. During the war, he had single-handedly captured two Pakistani tanks. One evening, a month before his retirement, he had set out for a stroll along the India–Pakistan border. Walking briskly, he had lost track of time, and in the spreading darkness, accidentally crossed over to enemy territory. The next thing he knew, he was surrounded by a group of Pakistani soldiers.

'Hands up!' they said, pointing their guns at him. They were planning to kill the infidel when the Pakistani major said: 'Wait! Let's have a look at the pig's face.'

Kuruppu shook with fear as several torches were shone in his face.

'Oh! It's Kuruppu sir!' The major knocked his knees and saluted him. 'Take him back immediately!' he ordered, and apologized profusely to Kuruppu. The soldiers lit the way with their torches and took him safely back to the border.

However, the handful of local ex-servicemen—they were a rare breed in those parts—secretly bad-mouthed him. They said he had no involvement with the military other than running the army canteen, and that the well-developed muscles on his shoulders were the result of kneading dough for the soldiers' chapattis. They implied that he was not eligible for the ration of alcohol that the army made available to all ex-servicemen. But Kuruppu was far superior to these people, both in ancestral wealth and bodily strength. He spoke better English and Hindi, and had developed salubrious relationships with more people in prestigious positions than they ever could. He took care not to speak much to anyone, and to suffuse the conversation with belligerence and disdain when he did. Acrimony was his natural disposition.

A skinny young boy from the neighbourhood came to look at the puppy. 'Da, patti,' he said, and poked it in the face with a stick. The puppy barked, making everyone step back in shock, then grabbed the stick with its teeth and looked cruelly at the boy.

'Her name is not "patti"!' Kuruppu gave the boy a hard tap on his head, and sent him off with a warning never to enter his compound again.

As the days went by, more and more people came to look at the puppy that had, by now, been christened 'Noor'. The relatives who came to see Kuruppu's newborn son showed more interest in the puppy that was the colour of polished mahogany, and spent hours watching her rest in her cage. Their experience with dogs, other than the local mongrels, was limited to the occasional Pomeranian, or in trying to imagine, on their way to the city, the breed of dog that produced the lion-like roars emanating from the palatial houses hidden behind high perimeter walls.

'This is a German Shepherd,' Kuruppu heard someone declare as he stood watching his wife and son from a safe distance, as demanded by customs of childbirth-related pollution. He did not feel the urge to pick his son up and hold him against his chest, and smell the top of his head. He was the type of old-fashioned man who thought such deeds unsavoury. He rarely even spoke to his wife in the presence of others.

'No, no! It's an Alsatian pup. You can tell by the black markings on its face,' said Kora sir, the lifelong president of the public library.

Kuruppu wanted to tell them that the puppy was, in fact, a Belgian Malinois, a breed classified as distinct from the Belgian Shepherd by the veterinarian Adolphe Reul around eighty years ago, and that there was only one other dog of the same breed in India. But what was the point in trying to enlighten a bunch of ignoramuses who did not even know that German Shepherds and Alsatians were, in fact, one and the same!

More things that would amaze Kuruppu's compatriots were yet to happen. A man named Beeran—they called him Beeranikka—cycled eight miles every day to deliver goat meat to Kuruppu's house. Very few among them had sampled goat meat as it was usually only available where there was a sizeable population of 'Kakkas', as Muslims were called locally. Only two Kakkas were seen in the area—one a trader who came to buy dried areca nut and the other a man who bought and sold old brass vessels. People called them 'Mothalali' as though they were big-time businessmen, purely because they wore wide leather belts that had pockets stuffed with currency notes around their waists. Beeranikka cooked the goat meat with turmeric powder on a fire outside the kitchen, under Kuruppu's watchful eyes. Noor could only digest tender goat meat. Kuruppu's mother, although not fond of dogs, made her wheat porridge cooked in milk. Noor ignored everyone except Kuruppu, and ate only what he gave her.

Meanwhile, Vasuvasari, the carpenter, dragged his left leg ballooned with elephantiasis to Kuruppu's house to build a kennel in the front yard. It was half the size of a bedroom. He had been out of work for two or three months, so he took his sweet time finishing the job, painstakingly turning the legs and sanding them to perfection as though he had forgotten that he was building a kennel for a dog.

'I wish I had been born as a dog in Kuruppu's house,' he told all and sundry at his job sites and at the arrack shop. The arrack vendor had dumped the day-old tapioca and fish curry in a plate outside the shop. A skinny mongrel was lapping it up, holding the plate down with its front paw. Vasuvasari, an incorrigible joker, bowed to it, calling it 'Guru'.

'He's the one who taught us carpenters our work,' he said. 'Look how he's holding down the plate with his paw to stop it from moving. Just like we carpenters sit on top of the wood we work on.' He stole a meaningful look at the shop owner's wife.

One morning, following the advice of the veterinary doctor who visited once a month to examine the puppy, Kuruppu set out with Noor in a taxi with national permit. By then she was a year and a half old. For a month afterwards, in the silence devoid of her regal bark, people gossiped about what had become of her. Even the local thief, Satyanesan, began to feel bad about the time he had tested Noor's mettle by chucking a boiled egg with a needle hidden inside in front of her.

When the car passed St Aloysius Church on Old Port Road in Mangalapuram, Noor looked at a two-storeyed house on the right and barked. She had been silent ever since they had left home. Filled with pride, Kuruppu lovingly scratched the back of her neck. In Tumkur, Noor was mated with India's first Malinois dog, the six-year-old Malswama, and on their way back Kuruppu stopped at that house. Noor walked right in as though it was her own house, and lay down under the bed. As she watched with interest, the normally stern-faced Kuruppu talked non-stop in English with Polly Mathew, the blonde-haired woman whose house it was, helped her make omelettes in the kitchen, and had energetic sex with her in broad daylight on the sofa. Eighteen months ago, it was after a meeting just like this one that Polly had given Noor to Kuruppu. She had come back from the Philippines the day before.

Now, a naked Polly walked up to Noor and picked her up. 'Her mother had two pups,' she said, sitting back on the sofa holding Noor in her lap. 'They looked exactly the same. My hand was shaking when I was making my selection. One was to live in splendour in America, and the other here in India, in this land of beggars . . .'

'This is also the land of strong men . . .' Kuruppu said, fondling the hair on his chest.

When Noor had her pups—four of them, all male—they too looked exactly the same. Still, Kuruppu felt that one of them was somewhat haughtier than the others. He was the first to open his eyes, and pushing the others out of the way, first at his mother's teats. Kuruppu resolved to keep him.

A friend of a friend of Kuruppu's, Dr Kamalesh, came from Ernakulam to fetch one of the others. The doctor was younger than Kuruppu had imagined, and his car seemed to leave a trail of fragrance and coolness behind. Kuruppu gave him a notebook in which he had written down the details of what to feed the puppy for the next two years. He also gave him the telephone number of a dog trainer in Madras. He had given the puppy a name he had come across in the morning newspaper—Candy.

Another pup was adopted by Roy, the nephew of Isaac Thomas, the district president of the Karshaka Congress. Roy had already found a name for him—Jordan, the country in which he worked. Roy tried to hand Kuruppu an envelope with some money in it, but he refused it with dignity.

Kuruppu named his favourite pup Arthur. He had a separate kennel made for him, and fed him special food and medicines to protect him against childhood problems. In the evenings, he let him loose in the compound and watched his antics with a heart brimming with pride and joy.

The retired deputy superintendent of police, Gangadharan, went to Thiruvananthapuram at Kuruppu's request on a secret mission. Within a week, a veterinarian, a good-looking man dressed in a white shirt and black pants, arrived at the junction asking for directions to Kuruppu's house. He sat in the front seat of a police jeep whose engine was revving as though it was an impatient beast kicking up dust. Two sub-inspectors sat behind him in a respectful manner, and behind them, two ordinary policemen in half-pants stood on the running board, hanging on to the bars. One of them made eye contact with the paan shop owner who quickly pulled the wooden shutters down and withdrew into the darkness of the shop.

After examining the unnamed puppy, the doctor and his entourage went ahead to camp in a house owned by Kuruppu in a coconut grove by the side of a lake. An old Mappila, well known for preparing wedding feasts in Christian households, had been at work in the kitchen for the last three days. He had prepared chicken cooked in a roasted coconut gravy, fried catfish, snakehead murrel curried with plenty of chillies and tamarind, and acchar with vinegar. More policemen arrived the next day, and they handed a letter of appreciation to Kuruppu, signed by the district police chief and sealed with the elephant insignia of the state of Kerala. Finally, after posing for a group photo with Kuruppu, they went away with the puppy. The next morning, the *Malayala Manorama* newspaper carried an item about the puppy with the title 'Victor Dons the Khaki'. The reporter had mistakenly identified the breed as Alsatian. Still, the article said the puppy would strengthen Kerala's police dog squad, and concluded with the information that it was Kuruppu, an ex-serviceman, who had donated the puppy in the service of the country. Someone cut out the news item and pasted it on the wall of the arrack shop where it would remain for years to come.

Kuruppu went to visit Victor once. The puppy had grown and put on weight from the steady diet of meat at the police camp, and was being sent to the Tekanpur BSF Academy in Gwalior for training. Victor barked at Kuruppu as though he was a complete stranger. His gleaming body and long, sharp fangs terrified Kuruppu, and he concluded that the dog had not recognized him.

But Victor was not the type to forget anyone he had seen once.

By then, Kuruppu had lost his beloved Arthur. A man named Kuttayi, a haystack builder by occupation, had kidnapped him. On that fateful day, Arthur, only a month old, had been busy attacking an immature coconut that had fallen on the paved lane in front of the gate. He had grown up faster than the rest of the three puppies, and had even started to bark at things.

'I'm taking him, you son of a . . .' Kuttayi had said, picking up the puppy by the scruff of his neck and stuffing him into a bag, while aiming a string of obscenities at Kuruppu and his mansion. 'I'll give him yours and my father's name—Adam.'

With a thin birthmark on the left side of his neck and a gait with arms swinging, Kuruppu's father Sankarappillah—locally known as Adam Sankarappillah—had resembled Kuttayi more than Kuruppu. Adam Sankarappillah and Kuttayi were proof of the fact that children born out of wedlock inherited more genetic material from their fathers than those born legitimately within the marriage bond. Sankarappillah had acquired the nickname 'Adam' after being caught running out of the back door of the convent, as naked as the day he was born. Adam Sankarappillah was said to have kicked his father to death. Like him, Kuttayi, too, had, in a moment of uncontrollable rage, dragged his on-the-record father, Avaraan, off his bed and stamped him to death. And although he did not emulate his birth father's proclivity for night-time shenanigans, he had abandoned his wife and now lived alone in a shack in some unclaimed land beyond the fields. He went to church only during the annual festival. Harvest time was the only time he was visibly happy. As though to establish his undocumented paternity, he cut down coconuts and the best bunches of banana from Kuruppu's groves in broad daylight. And whenever his heart brimmed over with sorrow, he got drunk, went to the gate of Kuruppu's mansion and hurled obscenities at the house.

Kuttayi tied Arthur—who was now Adam—to a poovarash tree by the side of the canal next to his house. When, unable to recognize it as food, Adam refused to eat the dried bits of tapioca he was given, Kuttayi yanked him up by the rope around his neck, held him dangling in the air, broke off a stick from the tree and beat him thoroughly, and then starved him for two days. By the third day, having endured the relentless night rain, Adam caught a fever, and half a dozen forward-planning blowflies arrived to buzz hopefully around him.

For the first few weeks, Dr Kamalesh followed the instructions written in the notebook Kuruppu had given him to look after Candy. He took Candy to the vet regularly, fed him vitamins and deworming medicines, brushed his fur and bathed him once a week. But as with many men who live alone, routine did not come naturally to him. He usually left Candy's lunch in a special dish in his kennel, but on the first day he returned to work, he forgot to do this. Still, when he came home in the evening, Candy hugged his leg and gave him a welcoming lick on his face.

'You just help yourself to whatever you want,' Kamalesh said sorrowfully, and from that day Candy stopped using the kennel. The good doctor locked him in the house when he went out, and Candy ate what he wanted from the kitchen, the same food that the doctor ate. The rest of the time Candy roamed around inside the locked house, examining the position of the furniture and committing to memory the unique fragrance of each and every piece of it. For years to come, Candy would not see the world beyond the walls of that house or a human being other than Dr Kamalesh.

When his regular patients asked after his family, Dr Kamalesh would tell them: 'I have only one relative. A brother—he is a dog.' Candy was not particularly smart or ferocious, but he was a loving dog. His life was good, except for a single incident when he lapped up the brandy Kamalesh had poured on the floor for him and fell unconscious.

'Don't worry about it,' the veterinarian patted a guilty, dejected Kamalesh on the shoulder. 'Alcohol doesn't agree with dogs. We're lucky he didn't die.'

Victor joined the seventh batch of trainees at the Tekanpur BSF Academy. There were twelve dogs in his batch, and the policemen who handled them trained with them. Victor's handler was Sundaran Nadar, a man from Kanyakumari district who had settled in Changanassery as a young man and joined the Kerala police. Seven of the twelve dogs were German Shepherds, one from Nepal and another from Sri Lanka. Two others were Rottweilers, and two were Labradors. Victor, the only Belgian Malinois, was the first of his kind to train at the academy. The day Victor arrived at the academy, the lead trainer, Yoginder Singh, made a call to the police dog training centre in Sicily, Italy, to learn about Belgian

Malinois. It was his alma mater and Donatello, the trainer there, was his guru.

Victor had some peculiar characteristics. The dogs and their handlers were to train together as one of the primary objectives of the training was to cultivate trust between them. But unlike the other dogs, Victor refused to work with his handler. They coaxed him with treats and then tried punishment, but he ignored Sundaran Nadar completely. It did not help that the poor policeman behaved like a servant in front of Victor, his cowardice barely hidden behind his moustache, while Victor, who was good at playing his hand cleverly right from puppyhood, accepted only Yoginder Singh as his master. Yoginder Singh was baffled at first, but soon realized that Victor was an extraordinary dog. Just like human beings, there were among dogs those who were unsurpassed, and a trainer considered it a matter of utmost good fortune to have the opportunity to meet one such. Released from his training duties, Sundaran Nadar wandered around the lanes and villages of Gwalior, wondering about his poor wife and children left alone back in Changanassery. When he eventually got back home after six long months, what awaited him was a suspension order based on a report Yoginder Singh, smitten as he was with his pupil, had written.

Victor completed his training in three months at the top of the class. The day before the class disbanded, a grand march-past took place in the grounds of the academy. With leather belts adorning their chests and necks, the dogs marched with their handlers and saluted Yoginder Singh who stood on the dais. For the first time in the history of the academy, a dog led the parade on his own, without a handler to control him. When he got to the stage, Victor stood on his hind legs and saluted with his forelegs. Donatello, the Italian guru of Yoginder Singh, was present at the ceremony to witness the event. He had accepted Singh's invitation and come to India for the first time.

Years later, Donatello would write in his book, *How to Train Police Dogs*: 'In the police dog training academy in India, I saw a dog as intelligent as any human being.' He was known to be a man not prone to hyperbole, and over the years, Tekanpur BSF Academy would receive many calls from dog lovers all over the world who had read his book, inquiring after Victor. Many years later, at Yoginder Singh's retirement function, the felicitation speeches would be peppered with the word 'Victor', and he would surreptitiously wipe his eyes. Over the years, he would regularly call Kerala and keep track of Victor.

'Each one has a different destiny, even if they are born to the same mother,' a fisherman told his friend as he rowed the boat back home in the early-morning light after a night of fishing. He picked out the rotting kuruva paral and orange bromide stuck in the net and threw them to Adam. The first time he ate uncooked fish, Adam suffered a terrible stomach ache, but now he was used to it. Growling at the darkness as though to ward off someone trying to steal the fish from under his nose, he gobbled them up. In his hurry, he gagged and lapped up his own vomit. Like the tortured animal, the fisherman, too, had many brothers, three of whom had government jobs and two others who were moderately wealthy. He did not have a close relationship with them, but he talked about them to his wife and children at least a few times in a day. And when he would pass the big house on the bank of the canal, he would tell passers-by, 'That's my brother's house', and watch the puzzled looks on their faces. He had carefully put aside a specially tailored shirt in anticipation of an occasion when he might be invited to visit his brothers.

Adam grew up slowly, half-starved as he was most of the time. All day, he ran around the tree he was tied to, and when night came he howled at the darkness. Without regular brushing or washing, his dust-covered fur matted and his flea-infested skin broke out in itchy warts and sores. He spent his time scratching and biting at his skin and, like a sanyasi in search of transcendence, chasing his own tail. The coir leash snagged the hair on his neck and left a bald circle. Worried that he might break loose from the rope, Kuttayi replaced it with a metal chain. It chafed against the bald skin and left sores that got infected and attracted worms and flies. Convinced that he would be dead before daybreak, Kuttayi dug a hole to bury him before he went to bed. But the Man in the Heaven Above had other plans, and by morning the festering wounds had healed miraculously.

Among the siblings, Jordan had the most uneventful, comfortable and easy life. He was allowed to roam free in the four-acre compound enclosed by a big boundary wall. No other house in the vicinity had such a large compound. The only passage out of it was at the back where there was an opening that led to the cardamom grove next door, but Roy had extended the boundary wall and closed it after he brought Jordan home.

Gorging on the plentiful food, Jordan put on weight and spent all day snoozing in his kennel. Roy's wife and thirteen-year-old daughter enjoyed even better food and put on even more weight. No one visited except when Roy was in town, so Jordan had no cause to bark. Still, like a shipwrecked sailor marooned on an island, he talked to himself whenever he felt that he was forgetting his own language. On the other side of the boundary wall, grown men who had never had a sexual experience knitted fantastic stories about the good fortune that a pedigreed dog living with two beautiful women with no men around enjoyed, but Jordan was unaware of such things. As he put on more weight, he began to spend the nights, too, in restful slumber in the front yard. A quiet, easy life, the utmost good fortune an animal could ever hope for—he had that. Still, every year, around August–September, he would be gripped by restlessness. Listening to the soft barks and romantic chit-chat of the ordinary mongrels on the other side of the compound wall, he would run around trying to find a way out that he knew did not exist. One night, he began digging a hole in the loose soil at the base of the compound wall at the back of the house. After four or five days of hard work, realizing that the granite foundation of the compound wall went deeper than he had anticipated, he began digging at a different spot. And when that attempt came to an end at a rock, instead of feeling dejected, he tried another spot farther along. He did not give up even when his toenails broke from scratching relentlessly at the stony earth. In those months, his appetite waned and he lost weight.

'What is wrong with this dog?' Roy's wife exclaimed, staring with puzzlement at the unfinished trenches all along the base of the compound wall.

On his next visit, Roy took his wife and daughter and set out on a little trip. Freshly bathed and with a new leather collar around his neck, Jordan sat in the back seat of the car. Beyond Kuttikkanam, seeing the mist roll down a hill, they stopped the car and got out. Jordan ran up the hill. He turned back and looked at the humans in his life, and barking his gratitude at them, he ran down the other side of the hill and disappeared. A week later, Roy brought home a Labrador puppy, and named her Sheba. He told his wife that he would have called it 'Solomon' had it been a male puppy.

It was with the capture of the criminals Krishnan and Karunan—twin brothers who were known as Cat and Mouse—that Victor became famous within the entire police force. Even their own mother claimed that she could not tell them apart. They had committed several burglaries and the occasional sexual assault. They did these crimes individually, but after carefully planning them together, so that, if one was caught, he could argue that the other was responsible. With the help of a skilful lawyer, they avoided punishment in several cases. The trials of cases where Cat or Mouse was the culprit created several dramatic and comedic moments in courtrooms, with their lawyer making fun of the police as well as the victims when they could not tell one brother from the other.

But their fortune began to change when they were arrested together during an attempted burglary at a jewellery shop. At the police camp, Victor committed to memory their separate and distinctive smells. And from then on, when they were arrested, it was possible to tell which one had committed the crime. Finally, they were sent to prison for a very long time.

Life at the police camp did not change Victor's peculiar attitude. He paid little attention to ordinary policemen, and only recognized those above the rank of circle inspector, responding to them as though he was their equal. He operated with complete freedom when he was part of an investigation. The image that came to people's minds when they heard the term 'police dog'—a dog straining forward at the end of a chain held by its handler—was simply not true in Victor's case. Instead, like a stern-faced detective, he performed his duty and went back to his post, and the policemen regarded him not as a dog but as one of them.

Although not quite demonstrative of his considerable skills, there was an incident that made him famous outside the police force. A newly appointed excise commissioner, a man who was keen to be known as someone who could not be corrupted, began the task of systematically destroying the marijuana farms hidden within the forests in the High Range hills. The raids did not get off to a successful start. Then Victor joined the effort, his keen nose following the scent of 'shivamooli'—as ganja was locally known—over several kilometres deep into the forests. The khaki team followed him, cut down the plants and set light to them. As they sat huddled in their tents in the piercing cold, they smoked the ganja they had cut down, and wondered why human beings were destroying the plants God had created in His wisdom. Walking around the forest, some of them witnessed a fantastic sight. Through the gaps in the tree trunks, they saw a dog that looked exactly like Victor, with a leather collar around its neck, pass before them. They would have mistaken him for Victor had it not been for the dire state of exhaustion he was in.

A government minister, pursuing the fame that would come with taking part in the raids, arrived at the police camp. The man, known to be a buffoon, was accompanied by a group of inebriated photographers representing a range of media outlets. One of the newspapers published, prominently on its front page, a photograph of Victor leading the minister through the forest, with the caption, 'Who is the smart one?' After this incident, when important cases were being investigated, people began to ask not whether they had brought a police dog, but whether Victor had arrived.

It was on a day human beings consider auspicious that Adam found his freedom. A mischievous young boy lit a firecracker and threw it at the tree to which Adam was tethered. Assuming it was food, Adam looked at the boy with grateful, unbelieving eyes and fell on it. In the shock of the unexpected explosion, he broke free of his leash and began running. It took him some time to realize that he was free, and in the delirium of that realization, he stuck his tail between his hind legs and ran around all over the place like a rabid dog. He bit two humans and a cow, and in the night broke into a toddy shop through its palm-leaf wall and ate the fish curry.

'My only relative is Candy,' Dr Kamalesh told the young woman who had come to him with a common cold, and seemed interested in him. The sorrow of having become a widow within a week of her wedding had left dark circles under her eyes, and she came often to the doctor with simple ailments or suspicions of ailments.

'Really? In that case, I'd love to talk to this relative.'

On their very first meeting, Candy understood that the woman was not a dog lover. Still, when she patted him on his back, he rubbed against her legs lovingly. She realized, with some amount of disbelief, that the man she had resolved to make her husband had been, for many years, sharing his meals with a dog and spending an inordinate amount of money on his upkeep.

Candy's misgivings proved to be true. On the evening of their wedding, she changed all the curtains and bed sheets that were covered in barely visible dog hair, cleaned the entire house, and shifted Candy back into the kennel that had been lying unused. Candy tried to establish a loving relationship with his new mistress, and, realizing that she did not like being licked or hugged, expressed his love by wagging his tail and growling softly. But what really worried Candy was that Kamalesh gave up meat and fish in solidarity with his wife's vegetarianism. He brought home a special package for Candy once a week, and Candy listened to the fights that ensued between the couple as a result of it.

Soon, they had children, and Candy watched as Kamalesh, too, began to grow distant. He stopped the routine six-monthly visits to the vet. Still, Candy's heart brimmed with joy every evening when he watched Kamalesh return from work in his car, and on the rare occasion, once a month perhaps, when he called to him lovingly, Candy forgot the neglect and jumped up to lick his face.

Despite his mistress's objections, Candy tried to befriend the children. They tried to lift him up with sticks poked under him, put stones in his mouth, and urinated on him, and yet Candy let them play with him like an adorable toy. Whenever they fell over or came to harm, he tried to bark to alert his mistress.

It was through the children's chatter that Candy came to know that Kamalesh had received a transfer order. He realized that his master was not going to take his aged pet with him to this new, faraway place. Only the youngest child seemed upset by this decision, and cried until he was pacified with a chocolate candy.

The day before their departure, Kamalesh and the children took Candy for a ride in the car. It had been a long time since Candy had been outside the compound, and he sat happily watching the world go by.

'You'll be happy here, Candy,' Kamalesh said when they arrived at the vet's house. He patted Candy, and as he kissed him for the first time in years, his eyes were wet. Candy watched until the car was out of sight, worrying whether the children would be safe in the new place without him to watch over them.

For the next two days, Candy was fed lavish meals in the new house. Although he had no appetite, he showed his appreciation by licking the hand of the woman who brought the food and barking gently.

On the third day, the vet came up to him. 'Candy,' he called softly, and stroked his face. He had a big syringe in his left hand, and Candy understood what was about to happen. He stared into the doctor's eyes and wagged his tail as fast and strongly as he could. As the medicine spread through his body and he felt himself slip painlessly into darkness, Candy continued wagging his tail. A few years later, someone would post his story, titled 'A Sad Dog Story', on the Internet and many people would admire it.

At the police camp, a young man they had arrested was stripped naked and made to stand, for the last three or four days, with his hands tied to a wooden bar above his head. He looked at Victor with begging, terrified eyes. Victor sprang forward from Inspector Janardhanan's hands. In the split second between him and the dog, the young man remembered his father and the girl who had been his first love at a tender age. Many years ago, he had written some political slogans on the walls of the school urinal—that was his crime. He confessed to the inspector that he had been inspired by the books he had read, and that no one else was involved. Inspector Janardhanan believed him, but he acted as though he did not because he enjoyed interrogating these hapless suspects, noting down the names they called out in the agony of their helplessness, and bringing those people too into the police camp within hours.

'Who needs clothes when they are in the presence of God?' Inspector Janardhanan told the young men tied to the table legs, window bars and pillars in the various rooms at the police camp. 'When you go to the temple, you take off your shirts, and when you're here, you must remove your underpants.' He had figured out that dogs were most useful in interrogations. Victor did not have to attack their exposed private parts. The sight of him was sufficient to make the suspects own up to their wildest fantasies. A few of them, like the young man who wrote the slogans in the urinal, would lose their ability to be aroused forever.

Everyone thought that there was a special chemistry between Inspector Janardhanan and Victor, while the policemen who worked with them suspected that Victor had some secret connection to a power centre beyond that of the police camp. The policemen who took his food to his kennel, which was always left open, did so with trepidation as they believed his displeasure could cause major problems. Every time Victor made his appearance at the police camp, which was an exhibition centre of impotent masculinity, many of the policemen stood up in respectful embarrassment. Even those who had a sense of pride found themselves unconsciously shifting in their seats. A policeman who was nearing retirement had to salute Victor for almost a month as punishment, meted out by the inspector, for daring to speak up for a culprit of his acquaintance who was brought to the camp for questioning.

Inspector Janardhanan enjoyed watching animals mate, perhaps an interest he had inherited from his father who was a breeder of herd bulls and billy goats. He found a young German Shepherd female named Lilith for Victor. Lilith was a year and a half old in dog years—around eighteen years in human terms. Although Victor showed no interest in her, no one questioned his masculinity because they knew he was a special type of dog, one who had complete faith in the infallibility of his species.

When people heard about the arrival of a dog catcher, they expected a middle-aged, hairy man with big arm muscles and a strong body. But the four-member team of dog catchers, equipped with ropes and gunny sacks, was led by a fair-skinned young man who looked almost as handsome as the film star Prem Nazir. They set up camp at the church-owned lower primary school, which was closed for the holidays, and slept on makeshift beds of benches pulled together. During the day, they roamed the land with their nooses, with a sizeable chunk of the local population, including small children, following them. They deftly lassoed the dogs they came across, injected them with poison, and buried the dead dogs after cutting off their tails, which they saved in their gunny sacks. Egged on by the enthusiasm of the crowd, they made up reasons to catch even pet dogs that had been lovingly brought up by their owners. Their ultimate aim was to catch the troublesome and clever dog named Adam. Never before had their bosses received a complaint where a feral dog with no owner had been named specifically as the troublemaker.

Adam had been using his new-found freedom to make up for all the years of starvation. Pushing open their flimsy doors, he entered kitchens and scoffed the food, scared the hens off their roosts and ate them, and hunted small goats, pet rabbits and ducks like a wild predatory animal. Within a few days, true to his pedigree, he had grown into a massive dog that no one dared to accost.

Finally, after many days of fruitless search, the four-member dog catcher team received news that Adam was hiding in a small islet made up of a few coconut trees and shrubs in the middle of a field. 'We'll be done and on our way back tomorrow,' they said. But that night, as they slept on the school veranda to escape the relentless heat, Adam and his friends set upon them, and by the time people heard the barks and screams and gathered with sticks and flaming torches, the dogs had done their job meticulously and were long gone. The four dog catchers were taken to the hospital in the nearby town. The handsome face of the young leader of the team was in tatters, his cheeks and ears shredded and his nose gone forever.

Victor received his second service medal for rescuing the inspector general (IG) who was attacked by a prisoner when he was on a visit to the police camp. Leaving the other policemen outside, Inspector Janardhanan and Victor had accompanied the IG on a tour of the rooms where the prisoners were held. An emaciated, half-dead prisoner had, with the unfathomable energy of an animal about to be slaughtered, jumped up from where he was huddled on the floor of his cell, grabbed the IG's neck and held on like a python from a nightmare. Shocked into inaction, all Inspector Janardhanan could do was to holler for the policemen outside, while Victor had, with great presence of mind, bitten the hapless prisoner's neck, pulled him down, mauled him and dragged him back into the cell.

One day, Inspector Janardhanan got word of a burglar who had been on his radar for a very long time, and a group of policemen, led by a sub-inspector and Victor, set out to apprehend him. The burglar was on the terraced roof of a concrete house—extremely rare in those parts—spending a few stolen moments with his beloved, gazing at the sky. As soon as he saw the police, he jumped off the terrace to the ground below, and Victor jumped after him. The burglar had his legs broken, and Victor broke his spine. The burglar spent the rest of his days begging in the streets, pulling himself around on a small wooden platform fitted with wheels. The inspector got a special wheelchair made for Victor, and the policemen who were out of favour with him found themselves assigned to the jobs of wheeling him around and cleaning his kennel.

Adam lived out the rest of his days in such a way that did justice to the original owner of his name. Perhaps because of the heroic act of getting rid of the dog catchers, he became the forever lover of the local bitches. They had never seen a dog with such valour of heart or splendour of body. His self-confidence was forged in the fire of the hardship of his youthful days. Not satisfied with his love life on the streets, he entered the houses secured behind boundary walls, mated with the pampered bitches inside, and even freed some of them from captivity. And as though to replace the dogs killed by the dog catchers, a new generation of stray, half-starved puppies with mahogany-hued fur and black mask-like marks on their faces began to appear all over the place.

Adam's luck began to change after he swam to the middle of a pond and rescued a drowning child. He was middle-aged by then. He did not have to break into kitchens any more. People fed him lovingly. Soon, the land was freed of the fear of burglars, and people slept peacefully through the night to the music of the frolicking new-generation puppies.

The morning after Inspector Janardhanan retired from service, Victor's lifeless body was seen hanging from a cashew tree beyond the parade grounds. There were signs of an attempt to skin his body and gouge out his eyes. The former police minister, who had by then lost his seat and almost ended up in prison, came to pay his respects. He stood before Victor's dead body, which was laid out with all honours, wiped his eyes and whispered something to the person next to him. Watching him, the people gathered there suddenly found themselves doubting all that they had heard about this obviously soft-hearted person.

Adam died in a manner befitting an honourable stray dog. He was run over by a vehicle on the highway about five kilometres to the east. Heavy vehicles rode over his carcass until he disintegrated into nothingness like a clod of mud in rain.

Kuruppu's son, Akhilesh, had gone to England for higher studies and then worked in Delhi for a few years. After his father's death, he resigned from his job and came back home. He lived in that empty house like a malevolent spirit, spending his considerable ancestral wealth in the pursuit of drunken parties. He brought home a stray puppy, and gave him the name 'Adam'. Even after six–seven generations, the puppy retained the mahogany colour and the black face mask of his ancestors.

'If you live like this, there will be nothing left of your wealth,' a relative admonished Akhilesh.

'I want to live like a stray at least for a day before I die,' Akhilesh said. He took a sip from the cocktail of black tea and rum, and stroked the new Adam on his back.

Adam ran to the front yard and fetched the newspaper. 'A Belgian Malinois dog, Cairo, joins American marines in the quest to assassinate Bin Laden,' the relative read the headline aloud.

Akhilesh smiled. 'He's a relative of Adam,' he said, thinking of his father, Kuruppu, an Anglo-Indian woman named Polly Mathew, and the litter of puppies she had considered in the Philippines, wondering which one to choose.

Adam ran out through a gap in the dilapidated boundary wall. The gang of puppies waiting for him outside howled in chorus as he joined them, and they ran around chasing and nipping each other playfully.

death notice

The pregnant cow—a hybrid variety—that lived in our old barn began to have contractions by 8 p.m. that night. A few hours before that, a mongrel bitch had given birth in the screw pine thicket behind our compound, her ear-splitting screams announcing the searing pain of her body opening up to the whole world. She was paying the price for months of canoodling, at the exact same place, with all kinds of dogs in the neighbourhood.

Within a short while, as directed by my mother, I stood in the pouring rain and dug a hole in the mud. I picked up the puppies one by one—seven of them in rainbow hues—and put them in the hole. With eyes that would never open to see the world, they grubbed around, searching for their mother's teats. Rainwater splashed as I filled the hole with mud.

'What sort of a mother are you?' I asked Amma after washing the soil off the spade.

Amma gave me a glass of tea, and took a plate of day-old rice and fish curry over to the heartbroken, moaning bitch that had followed me.

The cow's fate was entirely different. As soon as the labour pains started, Amma lit a kerosene lamp and sat beside her, scratching her jowls and stroking her head. She bore her pain proudly, with not even a whimper. Unfortunately, the calf came out feet first, and my worried mother promised an offering of a ghee-filled coconut to the god in Sabarimala if all went well.

By the middle of the night, I picked up an umbrella and set out, alone, to fetch the veterinarian, Krishnan Namboothiri. I had to cross a few small canals that filled with water only in the rainy season, and cut across a deserted banana plantation to reach his quarters which were a couple of kilometres away. I shone my torch into the canal to see whether fingerlings of fish were coming up with the rising water.

I knocked at the doctor's front door for a long time, and when it opened finally, it was not the doctor but a beautiful woman with thick, curly hair. Even her shadow seemed to be sparkling. I told her the reason for my visit so late in the night.

'Thirumeni is in bed,' she said, referring to the doctor with the honorific title reserved for his caste. 'Drank until he vomited. Won't get up now till it's time to go to the temple in the morning.'

'You must be his daughter,' I said, lying shamelessly.

She tucked a strand of hair behind her ear. 'No,' she said coyly. 'I am his wife.'

'Thirumeni was the one who gave the injection to impregnate the cow,' I said, pulling the umbrella shut and climbing the step on to the veranda. 'So much easier than in the old days when one had to search for a herd bull to do the deed.'

She laughed and went back inside the house, leaving the door partially open.

Human beings are strange creatures, I thought, as I walked home in the rain that had lost its vigour and become a faint drizzle, like chalk dust in a classroom. It was obvious that I was interested in her, and she in me. Then why didn't she invite me in? Why didn't I walk in through the door that she had suggestively left open? Oh, if only I had been born an animal! Never had a male buffalo been attacked by the brothers of a female of the species for showing sexual interest in her!

Lost in thought about how human beings had unnecessarily complicated the performance of a simple, basic human need, I came across what looked like a hunk of rock moving by the wayside. A turtle, a good-sized one, was swimming up from the rainwater spill. I had seen many floods and gone fishing several times but had never seen such a big turtle in my life. I picked him up, turned him over and held him in my right hand, lighting my way with the torch in my left. Like a newborn baby, he looked up at the lone star in the night sky and wiggled his arms, legs and head. My thoughts went back to the beautiful woman who was destined to live with a man who put his arm up the backsides of cattle for a living.

By the time I got back home, the cow was in dire straits.

'Nothing we can do now, Devakiyamme,' our neighbour Neelandan, who was an expert when it came to domestic animals, told my amma, carefully looking over the cow which was lying on her side with swollen udders.

'Her legs have given out. We can't get her to stand up now.'

Amma cried. The cow had been giving us milk for four years now. We had sold her once but she had come right back to us.

I fell asleep on the wooden bench on the veranda, trying to keep warm under a narrow blanket, and had a strange dream involving crying puppies and a beautiful woman. I could hear the sad howls of the bitch searching for her pups, sometimes in the yard and sometimes in my dream. So many deaths and a woman, all in a single night, I thought to myself as I slept.

Before dawn, Jose, the butcher, arrived with a couple of strong-bodied strangers, and dragged the cow across the yard and into the lane. They quickly loaded her into a truck and drove off before anyone could see them.

'She was so brave, but when they dragged her over that stone, she cried,' Amma said. Jose had given her five hundred rupees for the cow. 'If she had given birth properly, we could have sold the calf for at least five thousand.'

I got up late the next day, took care of some urgent matters, and when the rain ceased a bit, walked briskly towards Peter sir's house. The turtle was in a bag I toted in my left hand. This was the first time he was travelling through air. My feet sank into the soft, squidgy lane strewn with decaying leaves of rubber trees, and I had to lift them up with some effort. Last week when I had come this way, the lane was littered with rubber fruits bursting in the scorching sun. Since I was a man who liked to ruminate over things, I marvelled at the quickness with which people and the weather changed. Take Sreekala, for instance. About a month ago, while attending a funeral at a house, she had let me fondle her breasts. And then yesterday she introduced me to her brand new husband: 'This is a relative of mine. His name is . . .'

At Peter sir's house, we put the turtle in a pot of boiling water. 'Looks like he's laughing at us,' I said, watching the creature scurry around. This was the best way to kill a turtle and take its shell off. Some people sit on top of it and press down, and when it pokes its head out in pain, they put a noose around its neck and kill it. I have seen nomadic circus people and ragpickers roast it in its shell on a fire, and then there are the cruel bastards who insert a sharp knife into the side of its shell and cut it open when it is still alive.

'Not us, he is laughing at you!' Peter sir corrected.

A white substance oozed out from the turtle's shell into the hot water, and a smell of broiling flesh like in a cremation ground emanated from the pot.

'Your father's name was Sankunni. Do you know what your father's father's name was?' Peter sir asked me.

'Pappi, I think . . .'

'And his father's name?'

'I don't know!'

'Neither do I!' Peter sir said. 'But this turtle would have known him. Turtles live up to two hundred and fifty years. That's why he is laughing at you.'

Patting me on my back, he congratulated me for finding this elderly turtle. It was the Vaidyar, the local medicine man, who had prescribed this treatment for asthma.

'It is difficult to treat asthma when you're eighty years old. Only death will end the suffering,' the Vaidyar had told Peter sir. 'Try eating turtle meat. It might help. Cook it only with turmeric and black pepper.'

When Joppan chettan, Peter sir's help, began to prepare the meat, I sat on the porch, picked up the newspaper that was waiting silently and began reading it. A corner of the newspaper, where there was an item about a servant who had murdered an old woman and made off with her money, had torn off in the rain. I looked suspiciously at Joppan as he stood chopping onions, with a halo around his dark-skinned face, talking quietly to himself. Joppan chettan was a peculiar character. He had first come to Peter sir to help with looking after the nutmeg and coconut trees. The compound was overgrown with weeds and scrub because no one would work for long for Peter sir, who had strict rules and demands. So Joppan began cutting back the wild vegetation and digging over the soil. He did not waste time chatting or smoking beedis. When he reached the south-western corner of the land, he felt a weight on his hoe as though someone was pulling at it from under the soil. He dug deep in that spot and came upon a stone idol shaped like a snake.

'Your father, Manjappelayan, was also a Christian, wasn't he?' Peter sir asked him.

'Yes,' Joppan said.

'Then there's nothing to worry.'

As directed by Peter sir, Joppan put the snake idol in a gunny sack and took it to the west of the compound in the middle of the night. He recited a mantra and threw it into the canal.

'As if they can get the better of us Christians!' Peter sir said.

When Mary teacher, Peter sir's wife, passed away, Joppan got promoted into the kitchen, much to the amazement of his own wife who wondered what her husband, who could not even make tea, did in there.

Peter sir saw that I was reading the death notices in the newspaper.

'I only started reading this section after the age of sixty. You've started already?' he asked. 'One feels a sense of spirituality when one reads them, that there's only so much to life, just as when walking through the emergency department at Medical College Hospital.'

'I was looking to see who has won today,' I said. 'Today's winner is a Krishnapillah from Mulankunnam. He was 104 years old. And the loser is a Kichu from Erumeli. Only a year old. Death by misadventure . . . Fell into a well.'

Peter sir was intrigued by this game. I brought down a pile of old newspapers from the top of the almirah and began cutting out individual death notices from them. Peter sir joined me. I scolded him for sending the pair of scissors in his trembling hands over the dead in the pages and rendering around ten–fifteen of them useless. We put the rest of them in a cardboard box and sat down to play. Each of us put a ten rupee note on the table. I lost the first game. From the box, Peter sir picked up a Prabhavati, forty-seven years old, while my pick was a twenty-nine-year-old Unnikrishnan. Peter sir pocketed the twenty rupees. He won the next game too with sixty-three-year-old Eli, but in the third game I had an indisputable lead:

Kuruvila, ninety years old, against Peter sir's pick, Shaji, fifty years.

'He was my student, you know,' Peter sir said gleefully. 'A terrible sort. He had been in prison twice. Many years ago, when my car burst a tyre on M.G. Road, he came to my help.'

'Well, it's the sinners who keep this world going,' I said, picking up the notice and looking at Shaji's photograph. It was one of those studio photographs from an identity card, the official seal still visible. He was a mild-looking man, and his eyes reflected the lights in the studio where the photograph was taken.

'True, the baskets of the well behaved are always leaking,' Peter sir said.

'That's not what I meant. The well behaved just get on with their lives, while it is the villains and the scoundrels who prompt changes in the world.'

'I guess you're right,' agreed Peter sir. 'If the Devil hadn't interfered, we'd still be in the Garden of Eden, eating fruits and shitting, and wandering around naked.'

In the next game, much to my shock, I saw that the death notice I picked up from the box was my own. It baffled me, but I quickly put it into my pocket and smiled secretively. Peter sir also seemed to do some sleight of hand and smiled at me, which made me smile, which in turn made him smile again.

Winning three games in a row put Peter sir in an agreeable mood, and he went inside to open his fridge. He was, by nature, churlish, even towards the hapless beggars who came around occasionally, and I often had to find some way to mellow him out so that he would feel like sharing a bottle of something to drink from his stock.

'Last time you had arrack . . .' I said, looking dejectedly at the cheap bottle of brandy he placed on the table.

The other day, when Joppan fell out with him and left, Peter sir destroyed the pots and bottles he used to brew arrack, worried he would grass him up to the police. Joppan had a habit of taking off on some real or imagined slight only to return a week or two later, and Peter sir would wake up one morning to find him hoeing the compound as though nothing had happened.

'I've tried all kinds of alcohol, the expensive kind and the cheap.' Peter sir seemed displeased.

'All kinds? Even Johnnie Walker Blue Label?' I pretended to be sceptical.

Irritated, Peter sir got up and brought out a blue, imperial-looking box. Unlike other liquor bottles, it had its own lock and key.

'In the CIA, they celebrate the success of each operation with a bottle of Blue Label,' he shared the secret that his son who worked in the US Navy had told him. 'But this is not for you. An old friend of mine is coming to see me from Bhopal. He's a judge. I'll open it then.'

'A judge?' Having never seen a judge in my life, I was truly sceptical.

'Retired. Quite accomplished too. He's sentenced ten people to death.'

I hooted in happiness. 'Let me know when he's here. Not to drink with him or anything, just to see him.'

'He's very strict. And principled.'

Joppan joined us for the next game, dropping the only ten rupee note in his pocket on the table. It turned out to be a disaster. The death notice he picked up was of an unidentified corpse said to be above forty years of age. Peter sir got forty-two-year-old Krishnananda Pai, and I picked up Rejimon, thirty-five years old. At first, Joppan demanded victory, and then a draw, but Peter sir pocketed the ten rupee note and banished him into the kitchen. He left, his face dark with rage.

A few games later, Peter sir and I fell out with each other. I picked up Fousia, fifty-six, and he, fifty-five-year-old Anilkumar.

'Anil is fifty-eight,' he claimed. 'I know because he was a student of mine. The newspaper got it wrong.'

The argument went on until, in a fit of rage, I grabbed the box with the death notices and threw it out. The dead scattered, some falling in the front yard and others near the kennel. Unlike the mongrels who howled at the sight of the dead, the two dogs in the kennel barked, sonorous and dignified. The bark of the older dog, an Alsatian, echoed off the walls of the house and in the well. Peter sir was the first president of the local kennel club. He had certificates proving that his dogs were pure breeds going back eight generations. Even Namboothiri Brahmins could not produce such clean certificates of pedigree. Peter sir had once told me, scratching the German Shepherd's head lovingly, 'He is pure Aryan.'

My excessive behaviour enraged Peter sir.

'I came to know that you're a writer only the other day,' he said. 'If I'd known earlier, I would not have let you into my house.'

Still furious, he told Joppan chettan a story about how he used to send my father, who was his student, to buy alcohol.

'What sort of stories do you write?' His voice dripped with sarcasm.

'Fantasy, mostly,' I said. 'I don't show them to anyone.'

'What? Like the race between the hare and tortoise, and the story of the mud clod and the dry leaf?'

I was blown away by his ignorance. 'Those are not fantasies,' I said. 'Those are true stories.'

Joppan chettan nodded in agreement, and told us about the varaal fish he had met as a young man that had been almost as intelligent as a human being.

'So now I'm the crazy person!' spluttered Peter sir. 'What do you boys know about life? Have you even been outside of Kerala?'

'I've been to Kanyakumari and to Mysore . . .'

'You're almost thirty, aren't you?' Peter sir asked, pointing his walking stick with the gold-plated grip at my nose. 'Have you even been with a woman yet?'

He caught me winking at Joppan chettan who had come over with a plate of the fried turtle meat. Furious, he began pacing, his chappals making a squeaky noise followed by a clap as they hit against his heels.

A crow, bearer of ancestral souls, sat on the pomelo tree in the yard. 'See, he's waiting for you,' I said, pointing to it. 'He doesn't know that you are a Christian.'

The fight put me in a joyful mood because, when provoked, he would untie his bundle of old stories and place more bottles of alcohol on the table. He was the hero of many salacious stories that travelled from mouth to ear all across our village. We even had a saying—'like a house where Peter sir has been'—to describe disrepute. In people's reminiscences of their schooldays, he was either a monster from a nightmare or the object of extreme devotion. People above the age of fifty did not walk past his nutmeg orchard and front gate without deferentially lowering the second fold of their mundu. Like children peering into the tent of the snake charmer, they would turn their reverential gaze at Joppan chettan working in the yard and, sometimes, at me as I sat on the wall of the well, eating nutmeg skins dipped in salt.

Acting timid, I asked him the usual question that brought him out of his anger. 'Your students called you "Tiger", didn't they?'

Patting his grey moustache into shape, he sat down on the chair with a slight smile on his lips. He stroked his chest, the hair sparse and muscles sagging, and opened his mouth and took a puff from his inhaler. I had heard the story of how Muttan Sunny—a rowdy in Pala known for knife fights—had given him that name at least fifty times.

'Kids in schools were much older in those days, and there were strikes and agitations often. I didn't usually get involved because as soon as they saw me, they would disperse and go back to class. But one day, everyone ran away except for Sunny who stood there and continued to call out the slogans.'

Peter sir bent forward, and with the same force from forty years ago, he roared into my ear: 'Poda! Get to your class, now!'

A glass tumbler on top of the fridge jingled. In the few moments of silence that followed, only Joppan moved and continued stirring things in the kitchen.

Sunny wet his pants and ran back to class, Peter sir said. 'Every year he comes to see me, for Onam and for Christmas, with a bottle or two. He is too respectful to join me. He only stands aside and watches me drink.'

At least once a month, a posh car would arrive in a cloud of dust, bringing some big shot businessman or political leader to Peter sir. Joppan chettan and I would be banished on those days. Elsa chechi, a sixty-year-old woman who had been widowed at the age of twenty, would be in the kitchen, preparing pidi and chicken curry for them. When Mary teacher was alive, Elsa chechi used to help her in the kitchen.

Once, with some evil intent on my part, I had asked Elsa chechi: 'How is Peter sir these days?'

'It is good that the poor soul departed early,' she told me, thinking of Mary teacher. 'He's on his last legs. Still, it won't be easy shutting the lid of the coffin!'

'Why do all these people come to see you?' I asked Peter sir.

'The new deputy superintendent of police . . . You know what he said? That they become braver if they sit and have a drink with me. When he was my student, I boxed his ears with a pinch of sand between my fingers for good measure. The scar is still there!'

'Have you ever eaten game meat?' I asked my next usual question, winking surreptitiously at Joppan chettan.

'Have I? Ha! There's nothing I haven't eaten—deer, wild boar, wild buffalo, snake . . .'

'Even dog meat?'

'Yes, once . . . In Assam. It's like goat meat, only a bit tougher.'

'Is there no place you haven't been to?' I made my next move.

My question set him off again.

'What, you think like you I've been running around in my loincloth in this back end of nowhere?' he asked. 'Before I got married, I travelled all around India. Afterwards, too. With Matathil Shaji. We used to buy cheap, second-hand cars from Haryana and Kolkata, drive them all the way to Ernakulam and sell them for a profit.'

'Did you ever drive through the Chambal forest?'

'Chambal is not a real forest. It's mostly rocky hills and scrub.'

'So you must have seen Phoolan Devi, too!'

'You remember Raghavan who ran away? I saw him in Chambal around thirty years ago. Must be dead now . . . He was doing slave labour in a cotton farm.'

Last time Peter sir said he had seen Raghavan, it was in Bihar with a preacher.

'And in Europe you met a madamma who spoke fluent Malayalam, didn't you?'

'In Austria, yes, when I went with my younger son. There are barely any people there, only cars!'

'What did you think of Lakshadweep?' I asked, jumping straight across to the other side of the globe.

'Just like our Cherthala . . . Lots of coconut trees and sand!'

He watched me hand over a full glass of brandy with just a splash of water to Joppan chettan.

'There's only one place where everyone is equal,' he said and proceeded to recite a poem written by Amitabh Bachchan's father and explain its meaning to us Hindi-less ignoramuses.

'*Bair badhate mandir masjid mail karati madhushala* . . . Temples and mosques make people fight with each other while the wine bar unites them. That was a favourite poem of Chacha Nehru.'

'Which country has the most beautiful women? Lebanon or Egypt?'

This, my next question, had to be asked carefully. If he felt I was being impertinent, he would kick me out. If not, I could listen to some salacious stories, like the one about a journey he made from Bombay to Ernakulam in the company of seven beautiful women who were cabaret artistes. It was long before I was even born. Peter sir had accepted the responsibility of bringing them to dance at a friend's hotel.

'We didn't sell a single ticket,' he had told me. 'In those days, if people knew you were the type of person who went to cabaret shows, you wouldn't be able to find a bride. It was not half as bad as some of the things we see on the television these days. Still . . .'

But this time, Peter sir ignored my question. Holding on to his walking stick, he stood up and walked slowly towards the eastern room. The big cupboard with sliding doors in the room had belonged to Mary teacher. Leaning the stick against the wall, he knelt on the floor in front of the cupboard and opened one of the sliding doors with some difficulty. A cockroach landed on him, and he flicked it away with a shout. Extracting a bottle of wine, the colour of the evening sky, he got up and placed it on the table.

'This is the only bottle left,' he said.

Poured into the crystal glass, the wine foamed, thick and red like the blood of a young woman. I sank my fangs into the rim of the glass and sipped, sloshed it around in my mouth, and swallowed.

Mary teacher used to give bottles of her home-made wine to guests as gifts to take home. 'It is sweet wine,' she would say, 'let the women at home drink it. Even children can have it.'

'If Mary teacher were around, we could have eaten beef cooked with koorka with this,' I remarked, chewing on the tasteless turtle meat Joppan had cooked and spitting it out. Peter sir raised a corner of his mundu and wiped his eyes. It was the first time I had seen him cry.

'Sir, you are like Duryodanan,' I said, trying to change the subject.

'Well, he was a reprobate like me.'

'That's not what I meant. A good story needs good villains. Don't you think Kumbhakarnan is a more compelling character than Sreeraman?'

'So let's all be sinners then,' he said sarcastically.

'They say the whole city wept when Duryodanan died. And like him, you too have indulged in the finer things in life, eaten the best food in the world, travelled to the best places, stayed in palaces, had relationships with beautiful women . . .'

'So what? Look at me now. Joppan leaves by eight in the night. I take my medicine, and just when I begin to doze off by midnight, this house comes alive. So much noise like the doors are being kicked open and the attic is falling down!'

'Old houses are like that, no, sir? A scurrying rat, changing weather, everything sounds loud.'

'It's not that. Sometimes the doorbell rings, but when I open the door, there is no one there. The gate rattles like someone is shaking it, and stones are thrown at windows. All night dogs run around in the yard barking at the top of their voices as though they know an old man is in here alone, scared and crying.'

'Maybe we should inform the police . . .'

'What will they do? They can't come and stand guard every night. It's the people who hold a grudge against me. Cowards, the lot! Scared to confront me and have to stab at my shadow instead!'

Disbelievingly, I looked into the darkness outside. The frogs and crickets were silent; not even the flutter of a leaf.

Lighting the way with the torch Peter sir lent me, I walked back home. The sky was clear with no sign of rain. Leaving the shorter route home, I walked across the field, wading knee-deep in the rainwater, and sat with a troubled heart under a coconut tree, smoking one beedi after another until I fell asleep on the grass. At exactly 12 p.m., I jumped out of my sleep and walked back across the field. This time I did not need the torch as the surroundings were enveloped in bright moonlight.

Peter sir's house sat like a hunched animal with eyes that glitter in the dark. I threw stones at the round neon bulbs on the gateposts and broke them, ran at the gate and kicked it forcefully. I grabbed the bars and shook them until the aged screws began to come loose. A light appeared in Peter sir's room.

'Shhh . . .' I soothed the dogs that came barking up to me, and they slinked away to the back of the house with their tails between their legs and with a peculiar meowling cry. Leaving the torch behind, I jumped over the wall into the yard.

Through the air vent above the window, I saw Peter sir trying to load his gun with trembling hands. He was the only person in our village to own a licensed gun. I banged on the wooden pane of the window. Swearing at the top of his voice, Peter sir slammed it open and fired his gun into the darkness. Dejected, he held on to the top of the door and struggled to breathe. He was having an asthma attack.

'What's your enmity with the man?' Joppan chettan asked, coming up to me from behind and touching me on my shoulder.

'Nothing.'

'We're just helping him cross the bridge,' Mary teacher said.

She sat on the low wall around the front yard, smoking a beedi, looking exactly as she had a year ago when she died, the same face and the same innocent smile. The whole world was in a conspiracy against Peter sir, I thought.

'Well, this game won't end quickly,' I said. 'It takes more artistry to confront death gradually than just dying.'

Together, the three of us banged and scratched on the windows, and ran across the yard throwing fearsome shadows on the walls. Peter sir let go of his grip on the door frame and sagged to the floor where he writhed and curled like a dead worm. A stench of old faeces and urine emanated from him.

I jumped over the compound wall and set out in a different direction, mulling over all the things that had happened in the span of two nights and a day. From the top of a hill, at the distance of half an hour's walk, I could see the lights in the veterinarian's quarters. She was there, sleepless in her bed. I thought of flying across to her, like a bloodthirsty vampire bat.

murder at the culvert

On an intensely cold evening at the end of December, they got together as usual at the club, named after a white man, around two miles from Kaliyaar Estate. Many of the regulars had stayed away because of the thick fog and drizzly rain, and even those who had braved the weather had gone back home earlier than usual. The main room had plenty of empty tables, but they sat huddled around a table in a corner of the extension on the eastern side, talking softly over a bottle of expensive poison.

'We must unearth his secret today,' one of them said, rubbing his palms vigorously against the chill.

He was the shorter of the two, and had successful businesses in Kottayam and Ernakulam. His wife and children were abroad, and consequently, his life was as free and dangerous as a country with no government. He had acquired a level of fame within his circle of acquaintances because of a recent solitary trip to Thailand and the liberally embellished stories he shared when he returned, including one about a massage he received from a young Thai woman. And now, even the most measured of women shook with suppressed laughter when they saw him.

The second man, the owner of a bus service that monopolized the routes all across the High Range, grunted in agreement as though he had carefully thought about the matter.

'I've heard so many stories about him ever since I was a young man,' said the first. 'What a life!'

A pretty, foreign-made scarf was slung around his neck, but a pong of wet leather emanated from his sandals. It annoyed the second man, who was dressed in an expensive khaddar-silk shirt like the ones usually worn by wealthy men, and a mundu of such fine quality that those who saw him felt the need to rise from their seats in respect.

'Something significant must have happened for him to change like this,' said the second man, sounding uncertain. 'He seems to have been able to live two entirely different lives.'

Stories abounded about Thambi, the subject of their discussion, especially about the man he was thirty years ago. At present, Thambi lived a more or less monotonous life like everyone else. But thirty years ago, he was known around Kaliyaar town by the name 'Maadan', the same name that was given to a solitary tusker in the forest around. Just as the elephant would come out of the forest every two months or so to rampage through the fields and destroy shops and cattle barns, Thambi too would come into town, on foot or in a bullock cart, to wreak havoc. The moment they heard 'Maadan is about', people quickly shut their shops and disappeared without waiting to find out whether it was the elephant or the man.

One time, the Tamilian workers in the estate got together with a newly arrived labourer, a man who looked like a karimbhootham, a dark-skinned ogre, and set upon Thambi, attacking him from all sides like an army of ants.

'This will be the end of Maadan,' said those who watched the attack. 'He can't fight back. Look, he can barely get a foothold!'

Thambi had arms that reached well below his knees, with palms thick with calluses. He managed to free one of them and swing it like a spade. The Tamilians had to carry the karimbhootham, first hoisted on a bamboo pole and then loaded into a bullock cart, all the way to Thodupuzha, from where he was taken to a hospital in Kottayam.

The doctor, a native of Pooppara, examined the karimbhootham's shattered face. 'Don't lie to me,' he said to the karimbhootham's friends. 'I too am from the High Range. There's no way this was done by a human being. He must have gone into the forest and encountered a bear.'

It was this Maadan Thambi who had changed, overnight and for no discernible reason, and become an entirely different man. He was a loan shark but he stopped enforcing the pay back of interest. When some of his borrowers returned the money without being asked, he took back only the original loan. He gave up his goonda activities, and stopped beating people up and demanding protection money from businesses. His cruel face, adorned with an unruly moustache and stinking of stale tobacco, rearranged itself into one as tranquil as that of a bunny rabbit, and he began speaking in a low, mild voice. Instead of bothering people, he took to working on the three–four acre piece of land that he had inherited. He would wake up early in the morning to clear it to plant tapioca and sprout the rubber seeds he had collected from the estate in polythene bags. He also contained his drinking habit, and now indulged in only a couple of pegs in the evenings.

Big-time rowdies usually changed their ways only if something calamitous happened to them. Nothing of the sort had happened to Thambi, and people were suspicious of his apparent transformation. So, for quite some time, they continued to avoid him and shuttered their shops if they saw him in town. As with things they could not understand, they began spreading several stories about Thambi's transformation. One story was that, like his dead father, Thambi too had lost his mental balance. Another unbelievable story suggested that someone had castrated him as he lay unconscious after a long bout of drinking, and this story began to gain traction, at least among some people, when he continued to remain unmarried. It would be another two or three years before someone, a new rowdy coming up through the ranks, would be brave enough to confront Thambi. The younger man was said to have beaten him at a place near Thodupuzha, and people said that Thambi's reaction was to offer him his other cheek, which the newcomer slapped obligingly.

Thambi's transformation brought an astounding vitality to the whole area. The women of the land had been terrified of him although he had never taken out his thuggery on them. Mothers had been reluctant to send their daughters to the government school across the forest, and had refused to let them go out of the house in the dark nights even to urinate. But now, hugging bundles of schoolbooks to their chests, young girls were seen walking along the lanes. People were out and about even after sunset, and bullock carts loaded with agricultural produce went trundling down to Thodupuzha with no fear of hooligans. Eventually, the tarmacked road, with its buses and jeeps, extended into Kaliyaar and beyond, and Vannappuram became a new town. The two men who sat in the club chatting about Thambi were also affected by the changes. The first man went down the hills to Ernakulam and set up a small business which rapidly expanded, while the second came up the hills with his buses that plied all across the High Range routes.

'Do people really understand the far-reaching consequences of that incident?' the second man asked. Each time they got together, they discussed these events with a renewed sense of awe.

'Whatever happened to Thambichettan on that fateful day truly changed this land. If not, where would we be today? Kaliyaar town would still be terrorized by elephants and wild cats.'

As they had planned beforehand, they got up quietly and moved towards the table where Thambi sat alone. He was not wealthy or prominent enough to be a member of the club, but he visited it every evening, and sat nursing his drink—just the two pegs—for a couple of hours. The bar staff stocked Men's Club, a brand of brandy that not many people drank, just for him.

'Thambichetta, may we join you?' the second man asked. The residual terror from their childhoods, when this man was in the golden age of his thuggery, settled around them like fog. Deep within their hearts, they nursed the belief that the calmness of such men was not to be trusted. The first man remembered a dream from his childhood, of walking up to a sleeping wild animal to see it in close proximity.

'I still remember how you jumped down from the platform on top of that tree,' he said.

'And you floored that policeman with one blow,' said the second man. He poured liquor into a glass and placed it in front of Thambi.

'I don't drink much these days, boys,' Thambi said, ignoring the talk about his past. He had a small paunch and his hair was beginning to grey, but he still looked as strong as he had always been. 'Still, since you ask so nicely . . .' he said and picked up the glass. 'Who knows, I might have to beg you all for a drink in the future . . .'

When Thambi got up and went to the toilet, the second man quickly topped up his glass. They got back to the subject as soon as he came back.

'Tell us, Thambichetta, what's your secret?'

'What secret? I don't have any secret,' Thambi said, surprised. 'I've never gone after women. Guess it's too late for that now . . .'

'Not that, Thambichetta. About what happened on the night you turned your life around.'

'Oh, that. That's not a secret,' Thambi said, topping up his glass. 'That night Eesho came to me.'

'Eesho? You mean the man who puts up marquees for weddings and such?'

'Piss off, boys. I meant Eesho Mishiha, our Lord Jesus Christ.'

He had spent that fateful day in Kaliyaar town, he told them, where he had sat in the attic of the grocery shop, and played cards and lost. Nursing that anger, he had set out in search of Baby who lived in a hut by the canal side and whiled away his time smoking ganja. He had been on Thambi's radar for a while. As soon as he came up on him, Thambi grabbed the child in Baby's arms and chucked him into the canal. His wife, an emaciated woman who looked like dried fish, began wailing, and Thambi withdrew without doing further damage. He did not feel like going to the toddy shop that evening, and as darkness spread, he walked along the lane through the rubber estate. Rain fell, but only in the forest of rubber trees.

'I felt as though I was dead,' Thambi said. Patting the waist-fold of his mundu, he realized he had lost the little parcel of snacks he had bought for his mother somewhere along the way.

'I walked on and finally reached the culvert. You know the spot where Kuttappanasari died a long time ago? I saw someone, just a shadow, standing there in the rain. He clapped his hands and beckoned me.'

Thambi walked up to the man and lit a matchstick. The man's hair and beard were long and wild. As he peered into the stranger's face, Thambi realized he also had terribly bad breath.

'I'm really hungry,' the bearded man said. 'Could you give me something to eat?'

'You know what I'm like,' Thambi said to his listeners, poking the first man's elbow with his finger. 'I knew immediately who that was. There were so many Pentecostals and preachers in the High Range, and yet he had chosen me, a complete low life, to test. He must be up to something, I thought.'

So Thambi invited the man home, and as they walked along, they vied with each other not to break the silence.

When they got home, Thambi's mother scolded him. 'I've told you a million times not to drag these strays home,' she said. But Thambi gave the man his supper, rice and salted mango chammanthi.

'Anyone else would have asked, "Have you eaten?" Not this guy. He just sat there and ate the entire meal.'

Thambi gave up his bed to the man and spent the night on the floor. When morning broke, the stranger was gone.

'You see now?' he told his mother. 'If it were anyone else, would they have gone off so early in the freezing cold of the morning?'

A meaningful look passed between the two men listening to his story.

'Within a week, the old woman was dead,' Thambi continued. 'Served her right! Her brothers beat my father to death.'

'So . . . this man . . . he didn't say anything else?' asked the first man.

'No, nothing. He came, ate his food, slept and took off.'

'He must have been some travelling mendicant,' the second man could not stop himself from saying. Recalling

Maadan Thambi's notorious days of violence, his friend kicked his leg under the table, warning him to keep quiet.

Thambi sat silently for a while. Then, in a voice suffused with anger, he said: 'You boys were not even a twinkle in your fathers' eyes when I had the whole of Kaliyaar town under my thumb. I don't care if you believe me or not. But if you want evidence, come, I'll show you.'

The three of them squeezed into the broad driver's seat of Thambi's autorickshaw, which had a flatbed at the back. Usually used to cart food for his pigs, it stank of decayed vegetables and scraps from the chicken stall. Despite Thambi's efforts to control it, the vehicle screeched and shuddered in and out of the potholes on the road. In the dim light of the evening, watching the pitted road filling with water in the pouring rain, the men felt that Thambi was taking them on a journey to hell. The crucifix hanging above the steering wheel swung crazily each time the vehicle juddered. Was this the same Thambi who was carried ceremoniously in a palanquin by the feudal landlords of Kuttanad to beat the agitators into submission during the Thoppipala strike? The first man took a surreptitious look at Thambi. He was older, yes, but his lean body was still that of a man in his prime.

A group of policemen from the Vannappuram station, waiting by the side of the road to conduct spot checks on passing vehicles, ignored them. The newly appointed sub-inspector had been informed by his constables that there was no need to check the sobriety of such a saintly person as Thambi.

Thambi's house was an untidy structure with extensions and embellishments added willy-nilly over time. He led them through a rabbit warren of rooms, switching on the lights as he progressed, into an interior one. A mat that looked like it was never rolled up was spread on the floor, anticipating sweet slumber. Thambi opened a wooden almirah, took out a medium-sized framed photograph, and wiped the dust off it with a wet palm.

'There you go,' he said, passing it on to the second man.

In the faded photograph, Thambi, thirty years younger, stood next to a primitive-looking bearded man. The second man studied the expression on the bearded man's face. He looked bored, as though he had seen many cameras and was used to posing for pictures. It was an unusual expression for people of that time.

'That day, after serving him food, I ran to the stables,' Thambi said. 'A Tamilian named Vellappan used to work there, and he had a camera. I brought him over and asked him to take this photo.'

The second man handed the photograph to the first man, who, although bewildered at first, looked at it and nodded.

Thambi offered to take them back to their homes, but they insisted on walking, saying that the rain had stopped and a brisk four or five-kilometre walk in the night was good for the constitution. As soon as they were out of sight of Thambi's house, they stopped and burst out laughing. They guffawed, rolled on the ground holding their stomachs, sat up and hugged each other, and laughed like they would never stop.

'See, that's all there is to it,' the first man said eventually. 'We think these people are something special, and they turn out to be complete idiots.'

'He sees John Abraham and thinks it's Jesus Christ!' exclaimed the second man.

'Oh, you're an even bigger idiot,' said the first man. 'That's not John Abraham. That's Sukumara Kuruppu. Many years ago, he killed a man named Chacko to fake his own death for the insurance money, and has never been caught. Everyone knows he was in these parts for a while, hiding in a forest officer's house.'

'No! That's John Abraham, the film director who made movies like *Amma Ariyan*,' the second man insisted. 'He started the Odessa Collective that raised money from the public to make films. Everyone knows he had come here to collect funds from the estate workers.'

They argued diligently for a time and then came to an agreement.

'Doesn't matter who it is, really. John Abraham used to work at the Life Insurance Corporation of India before he began making movies, and Sukumara Kuruppu tried to embezzle money out of an insurance company. Crooks, the both of them! One tried to swindle folks into giving him money to make movies, and the other killed a lookalike to fake his own death and claim insurance money. Either way, it was not Jesus Christ!'

Laughing and holding on to each other, they walked on. At the base of the hill was a house, known locally as Ammini's Bar, which sold home-brewed arrack and wild game, both illegal. The men felt that a visit to the joint was an auspicious end to their eventful day.

'Amminiyechi,' the first man called out, sitting down in the veranda. 'Get us a couple of halves.'

Mirth bubbled out of them as they continued talking about Thambi.

'If only people knew the truth . . . Imagine!'

'He'd be the laughing stock of the town.'

'Like in the movies. Villains always turn out to be buffoons in the end.'

They finished their drinks and walked on, eventually coming up to the culvert.

'This is where Thambichettan met Jesus Christ.'

The place looked frozen in time, as though the passage of thirty or forty years had been inconsequential. The first man sat down by the culvert where, all those years ago, the carpenter Kuttappanasari was found dead. He picked a leaf off a foul-smelling plant, the last of its lineage, and smelled it.

They howled into the night and listened to the echo, and urinated into the water flowing from the culvert. Shaking a wet sapling in the darkness, they made it rain again.

'Still, how stupid are you!' the second man made fun of his friend. 'Looking at John Abraham's photo and thinking it is Sukumara Kuruppu!'

'I've met Kuruppu in person,' the first man countered, angrily. 'My mother's house is in Harippad where he was from.'

'Yes, well, I've stood right next to John, like this! My father had a share in his movie.'

In that deserted spot, without anyone to bear witness, the argument heated up. They called each other names. The second man accused the first man's wife who worked abroad of being a prostitute. The first man called the second man's father a homosexual. They expressed doubts about each other's virility. Finally, John Abraham picked up a large stone and bashed Sukumara Kuruppu's head open with it, and bewildered by his action, ran away into the darkness. It was the first serious crime in the area ever since Maadan Thambi became a law-abiding citizen. As the crime was taking place, Thambi was fast asleep in his room, by the old photograph in which he stood next to a bearded man. A hiccup, the result of overindulgence after years of judicious drinking, rose from him.

magic tail

'Edee! Neethu! Pooy . . .'

Bineesh jumped out from behind the handcart of guavas as the vendor sprinkled chilli powder on the cut fruits. It brought a smile to Neethu's face even in the midst of her crying. A long time ago, he had jumped out in front of her exactly like this with a small knife in his hand because she had written down the names of the pupils who had talked in class and given it to their teacher. That time, she had laughed looking at the open fly of his buttonless half-pants.

'Don't laugh,' he said, and touched the front of his jeans. 'This one has a first-class zipper.'

Neethu refused the piece of guava he offered. He persuaded her into one of the least crowded bakeries in the Majestic area, and ordered two glasses of pineapple juice. As the heat increased, people came in and sat panting at the tables. Lonely middle-aged men struggled to look away from the tables where young men and women sat together, regretting, perhaps, that they had failed to be adventurous even once in their lives so far. One of them shouted angrily at the young waitress, whose only privilege was the glory of her youth, who served him his juice. She had just been discussing with her friend the weird behaviours that men over the age of forty seemed to develop.

'What's up with you?' Bineesh asked. 'Do you have conjunctivitis? Or fever?' He tried to contain his surprise at how much she had changed in the last eight–ten years they hadn't seen each other.

'Papa passed away last night.'

'Aren't you going home?'

'He's been here with me for the last six months. Keeping me company. The body is at St Mary's. I have to take it back to Kaipuzha.'

'Then do it,' Bineesh stood up. 'Who's here with you? Has anyone come?'

'No, it was just us here. My two uncles will land at the airport in Nedumbassery only tomorrow morning.'

Neethu told him all about her efforts since that morning, almost as though she was talking to herself. An ambulance driver she had approached had asked her for eighty thousand rupees to take the body to Kottayam. As a matter of fact, not one person she had approached had quoted anything less than seventy-five thousand rupees. She could take a flight but it would take at least two days to arrange to have the body booked into the cargo. As for other vehicles, the local people refused to transport dead bodies in them.

'Bastards.' In peppering his speech with swear words, he was exactly like his father, Damu. 'The other day, when two Telugu men died, our government paid to have the bodies taken back to their place, but when they got there, those who had accompanied the bodies got thoroughly beaten up by the local people,' Bineesh said.

'Aren't you a nurse in a hospital here? Don't they have an ambulance?'

'Just the one,' Neethu said. 'And that's gone to Mercara. It may or may not get back by tomorrow. Besides, the management can't stand those of us who are here on work bonds.'

'Ah, behold the glory of the Kannadiga land,' said Bineesh in Tamil. 'So, in short, you need the services of a smart, capable young man, right?'

'Yeah, well, don't be too eager to offer your services,' Neethu retorted.

By evening, Bineesh had turned an old Maruti Omni into an adequate hearse. He put the back seats down, bought a few bottles of perfumes that God had created especially for the dead, burners for frankincense and sambrani sticks, and tied a piece of black cloth to the front of the vehicle as a warning to worms and weeds and other worldly creatures.

'There are things that become useful only when we are dead,' he said. 'Reading the *Puthen Pana* and decorated umbrellas for you Christian folk, raw rice and darbha grass for us Hindus. We all have our insurance policies!'

When she saw the vehicle prepared for her dead father, Neethu wept recalling the hearse, meant for the destitute, left abandoned and exposed to the elements near the Kaipuzha church cemetery. It was the type that needed to be pulled by hand, and had a brass bell at the front and a few words of God rejoicing in the misfortune of humans painted on the sides. When her papa had lost his company job and sat at home, she had dreamt that her mummy played 'Sat' around it, sold vegetables sitting on top of it, and that it rolled uncontrollably down an incline. These days, the only people who found a use for it were the grandfathers—so old that they looked as though they were born 500 years ago when the church itself was built—who stored their hoes and baskets in it.

Waiting to get the death certificate from the hospital superintendent, Neethu felt dizzy. She had not eaten the previous night. The superintendent wanted to know why they needed a certificate to transport a dead body. Wouldn't people know that it was a dead body by looking at it?

'But they won't know if it had been murdered, would they?' Bineesh asked.

'We need another person,' the man who stood by the mortuary door said. He held the five hundred rupee note that Bineesh gave him to dress the body against the light and examined it carefully.

'Remember our neighbour Ayyappan?' Bineesh asked, holding his lips way too close to Neethu's ears. 'This was his job at the Medical College. Even now, if he is one of the servers at a feast, some people refuse to eat.'

In the surge of happiness in being able to arrange a mobile mortuary, he had indulged in a couple of drinks.

'It is in fact like you said to the superintendent,' Neethu said as the van waited in a traffic jam on Goodshed Road. 'I did in fact kill Papa. I forced him to move here, and as soon as he arrived, he began to suffer from breathing problems.'

Bineesh stopped the vehicle at the railway station and tried to persuade Neethu to take the Intercity home. It would reach Ernakulam in the morning, and she could take a taxi from there the rest of the way. He would be right behind her with the van, he promised.

Neethu refused. 'I want to sit here talking to you,' she said. 'Otherwise you'll fall asleep and two dead bodies will reach Kaipuzha tomorrow.'

'You know what could happen when you travel alone with a strapping young man. The whole journey is through deserted areas and forests. And he is in a box, helpless,' Bineesh said, pointing to the back of the van.

'But I know that you're a wimp,' Neethu retorted. 'I have nothing to worry about.'

'There's a quicker route once we get to Hosur, just about right for this vehicle,' Bineesh said, enthusiastically turning the van. 'We'll get some food there—some chapatti and chicken kebabs perhaps.'

The van raced along, leaving behind high-rises, and bit by bit they fell silent. Like an ancient spacecraft that had travelled across all the stars, it moved into a deserted landscape, through scrub, woods and rock formations. Every now and then, an animal stood, for a split second, dazed in the middle of the road like a sinner in front of God, before scrambling out of the way into the darkness. Realizing that she was feeling sad not for the dead man but for herself, Neethu began weeping again.

'Let's tell some salacious stories,' Bineesh said. 'Tell me about the Christian nurses you work with.'

'Shh . . . Papa is right there,' Neethu said. She observed with interest the movement of Bineesh's mouth as he chewed on something.

Farther ahead, the condition of the road deteriorated, and the vehicle rocked as it rolled noisily over stone after stone.

'We're really brave, you know,' Bineesh said. 'If we break down, we'll have to wait here until morning. If the generator runs out of power, your papa would be a real concern. And anyone coming by this way would be more interested in you.'

He stopped the vehicle and opened the rear door to check on the box. In the milky light, the man who had been known as Mattathil Kuriakose lay with his mouth open, displaying his teeth in what could be misread as a smile. Someone had tried to close his eyes that had frozen open in the intense pain he had experienced as he died. Dressed in the white mundu and full-sleeved shirt Neethu had bought, he looked more distinguished than he ever had in his life. Bineesh and the man who helped him at the mortuary had to cut the back of the brand new shirt open in order to put it on the cold, stiff body. Wiping the glass on the lid of the box for no particular reason, and touching the generator to check the heat, Bineesh climbed out of the van.

'I'll tell our kids not to keep me in a freezer no matter what happens,' Bineesh said, back in the driver's seat and starting the engine. 'There were some other bodies in the mortuary—all shamelessly naked.'

'Our kids?'

'Yeah, the children we'll produce, together.'

'But we're not going to get married.'

'One night together is enough to produce children. How long can a cat sit quietly watching the sardine frolicking right in front of it?'

'That happens only in films and the stories of Josy Vagamattam.'

In Hosur, Bineesh parked the vehicle behind a busy row of night shops. He stepped out after locking Neethu inside the vehicle, and came back half an hour later with a food parcel, three bottles of wine and bottles of mineral water. Neethu went to the rear of the vehicle to look in on her papa. Opening the lid of the box, she straightened his clothes, sprayed a little perfume, and lit the frankincense. She noticed with a sense of amazement that she did not feel like crying.

'Your papa and I got drunk together once, at a wedding in Uzhavoor,' Bineesh told her. 'He was quite funny.'

They had resumed their journey, and the van was once again travelling through what looked like a forested area.

'I told him all about how I tried to woo you while we were in school. He laughed so hard. Christian fathers are so laid-back and jolly.'

Neethu took a mouthful of the wine. 'Like sweetened arrack,' she said, and spat it out.

'Don't drink,' Bineesh grabbed the bottle. 'You girls make a mess when you drink. Or sleep like the dead.'

'Pull over.'

'The next stop is in Salem,' Bineesh said, excited that they were finally on a good stretch of road. 'We should fill the petrol tank when we get there.'

'I have other needs,' Neethu said. 'Didn't think when I drank a whole bottle of water.'

'I'll come with you. What if a snake bites in inappropriate places . . .'

'No need,' Neethu said, pushing the wing mirror inwards with a sly smile. 'You can sit right there.'

She was back within a minute. The road stretched in front of them, haunted and deserted. Tired after a relentless day, Neethu tried to curl up in the limited space of the passenger seat. Her shampoo-smelling hair had become frizzy in the dry wind, her body sticky with sweat. She looked at her feet in the dim light of the vehicle and saw that they were covered in dust and had become the dirtiest they had ever been. She tried to close her eyes and fall asleep, but sat up again when she could not. Bineesh dabbed at her face with a wet towel, offered to give her a good wipe down.

'It's boring once you leave Kerala,' Neethu said, looking at the unchanging scenery. 'It's just flat and endless . . .'

'But it gets interesting in one aspect,' Bineesh said. 'Women become different when they leave Kerala. Once past Walayar and into Tamil Nadu, you people are unstoppable, and once in Bangalore, there's no saying what you'll get up to.'

'Not me,' Neethu said. 'My behaviour changes once I am in Kerala.'

'Well, that's my only hope now.'

Bineesh swerved away from an old monkey sitting sleepless in the middle of the road.

'Eda, Kapish!' Neethu called out, and, forgetting the circumstances completely, laughed loudly. Until that moment, she had forgotten the nickname Bineesh had been given in school—Kapish, the name of the monkey with a magic tail that could be extended or shrunk as he wished, from a children's cartoon series. Despite having grown up, the old nickname brought out the monkey god Hanuman in Bineesh's features.

Angrily, he tugged the back of his jeans down and showed her his behind. 'Look, here's my tail.'

'Our classmate Smitha was convinced that you really had a tail.'

'Where is she now? I'll go and show her my actual tail.'

For the next several minutes, Bineesh sat quietly stewing in his anger. The silence brought sleepiness to his eyes.

'Damn, I am seeing double,' he muttered.

An old man rode a bicycle weighed down with something to be sold in the morning market. Watching his shadow, Neethu began to cry again.

'I could have been more loving towards Papa,' she said, not really addressing Bineesh.

At the checkpost, an officer examined their paperwork and put his head reverentially inside the van. It was the first time he was dealing with a vehicle crossing the border with a dead body inside.

'Was it an accidental death?' he asked in a respectful tone. 'Drive carefully. There was an accident just half an hour before.' Ceremoniously, he shone his torch inside the vehicle.

Farther ahead, Bineesh pulled up at the side of the road. Having woken up before the sun, some houses stretched their backs. The smell of idli wafted out of the kitchens of those who had to catch the early-morning trains to their jobs.

Bineesh shook the sleeping Neethu. 'I need to shut my eyes for a bit. Just fifteen minutes. I'll be okay then.'

He tried to sleep leaning towards Neethu's seat. The seat was wet from the spilled water bottle and, irritated, he moved around trying to find a comfortable position. As he began walking along the edge of a dream, Neethu lifted his head and placed it on her lap. Comfortable and peaceful, he lay thinking that he was at his energetic best when confronted with women's sorrow. He inhaled the smell of orange peel as the fullness of her body brushed gently against his face. She caught his wayward hand as it strayed towards other, more beautiful places.

'I thought I was dreaming,' he said.

'You're not awake yet,' Neethu said, fastening the buttons on her blouse. 'Men do all sorts of things when they are half asleep.'

A considerable number of people attended the funeral of Mattathil Kuriakose. Many of them were strangers to Neethu and had come when they heard about the death. They stood around in the compound and the yard declaring that although prone to playing the fool, the deceased had been a helpful sort of person. Relatives praised Neethu's courage.

The local Asari and Chovathi women expressed concern about the daring and self-reliance that Christian women seemed to develop from a young age. Traits that made them leave their children with relatives before they were a month old to board an aeroplane all by themselves to travel to Australia and Ireland to work.

Two of Neethu's cousins took Bineesh to the lean-to and got him drunk. 'Your sister is phenomenal,' he told them as he fell semi-conscious on to the bed. 'She was something even when we were in school.' The three of them roared with laughter at that.

Groups of nuns came and prayed loudly as the destitute, the old and the disabled in the orphanages they ran queued up tidily to view the body. The priest realized the importance of the occasion and obliged by reducing his eulogy to five minutes. His words were dazzling enough to encourage those who stood around to imagine the scene of their own death with some sense of conceit. Looking into the coffin, they felt that death elevated a person's self-worth.

When she saw Eli valiamma, a sort-of-sister of her dead papa, Neethu could not hold back her tears. The childless, ninety-three-year-old woman spent her days waiting for special occasions in her relatives' houses. Not one of their relatives had gone to their final resting place without receiving a goodbye kiss from her. She stood beside the body dressed in a freshly laundered white mundu, its edge pleated into a fan tucked at the small of her back, holding a neatly folded handkerchief. Unfolding the handkerchief halfway, she bent forward to place it respectfully on Kuriakose's face to kiss it. But she stepped back quickly, looking anxiously around to see whether anyone had noticed how she had scrunched up her nose. Watching her, Kuriakose's older sister's son Jose, who was a military man, also stepped back. He had already noticed that his hand had touched some viscous fluid as he helped move the body from the freezer that had not been working properly.

Neethu shook Bineesh's body sprawled all over the bed and woke him up. A ripe smell emanated from his day-old clothes and the alcohol as well as the sheet someone had covered him with against the recent rain.

'The rest you can give me later,' he said as he pocketed the money Neethu handed him, having given her a full and detailed account of petrol charges and other expenses. 'It needn't be in the form of cash. If you delay, you'll only find it difficult to pay the interest.'

'I am a cheapskate,' Neethu declared.

In a single manoeuvre, Bineesh had the vehicle on the road as neighbours and relatives busied themselves gathering the chairs and taking down the marquee. Neethu watched the westering sun and felt that it was neither day nor night. As the vehicle splashed up the rainwater on the dirt road, a magic tail extended out from its back and wound itself around her waist.

kavyamela

When I first became acquainted with Soordas, I was living under the name Vasuvannan, running a biriyani shop in a place that was neither a village nor a town at the edge of Dindigul. My shop had a name board with 'Hotel Anandabhavan' and 'Dindigul Thalappakatti Biriyani' written in Tamil and English in letters larger than the shop itself. Strings of decorative bulbs lit up the name board in the evenings. In order to hoodwink customers into thinking I was a direct descendent of the Naidu who began the tradition of Thalappakatti biriyani, I tied a long cotton towel around my head. The towel concealed my rapidly progressing baldness, and I also used it to wipe my dirty hands.

By around 4 p.m. when I would have some spare time, the most troublesome of the few Malayali young men who attended the Chechiyamman College across the road from the shop would come in, and watch me slice, at lightning speed, the onions for the next day's biriyani. I would swipe a rag over a table, disturbing the house flies, and they would sit there happily playing cards. Sometimes they would pool their money together and give it to me to procure them a bottle of alcohol. It was good to make friends with people younger than oneself.

Still, when they would start talking about the young women who were their classmates, a tremor would rise up from the earth through my body and into my head. I would rinse off the soap I used to remove the smell of ghee from my hands and rush towards them in anger.

'What the hell have you all come this far for? If you wanted to chase after women, why didn't you stay put at home? Is there any shortage of lovely, butter-skinned women beyond Kumali?'

Glancing at the photographs of the goddess Chechiyamman and Our Lady of Good Health at Velankanni, and of Ettumanoorappan keeping them company on the wall, I would continue: 'I too came here to study at this college, and look at me now! Don't let me catch you talking about women here again.'

Hooting with laughter, the youngsters would press me to repeat the story. My life was a cautionary tale that passed from batch to batch of Malayali youth who studied at the college, duly embellished in each telling with spicy details that even the hero of the story was unaware of.

As is wont to happen with such tales, I have forgotten how it all began. I lived in the college hostel, and in the evenings, I would come to Vellayamma's paan shop that stood at the spot where I now have my biriyani shop. Occasionally, her daughter Selvi would be at the shop, helping her chop the chewing tobacco. I wanted to give her the banana chips and chakkavaratti that I brought from my home back in Kerala. Within a few days, one night, Selvi let me in through the back door, and I went in with the anxiety of a first-timer.

'The next morning there was a wedding right here. The joyful bride was all decked up with marigolds in her hair. The bridegroom—me—had been tied to that tamarind tree over there all night.'

'You could have taken off later, no?' everyone asked at this point in the story. 'No one would have known.'

'The next time I saw Kerala was after I had two children,' I would tell them. 'And that too with two of Selvi's uncles keeping an eye on me, armed with the type of swords you would see in a Sasikumar movie. I should have spent my life married to a Chovathi or Nair woman, but instead here I am with one who bathes only on rare occasions!'

'So what if Selvi chechi is dark-skinned? She's gorgeous even now . . .'

'With that one night, my happy sex life was over. Now it is like the last meal of a man going to thc gallows in the morning.'

When the college closed for Pongal holidays, with no youngsters around or biriyani to make, I was whiling away the rest of a pointless day after a meal of a watery curry of cheera and parippu over white rice made by Selvi. My head supported by my left arm, I lay on a bench in the shop for what seemed like an eternity. The road was dead with no vehicles. Sun and shadows alternated, and on the neem tree outside, fruits set, ripened and fell off. A young man stood on the road, facing the shop and holding a white stick in his hand. The stick, the mistakes in the way he had tucked his shirt into his trousers and folded up its sleeves, and his face that seemed to be smiling even when he was not smiling, gave him away. He was blind.

'Do you know who sang that song?' His question was aimed at me.

I realized that he had been standing there listening to the song from the radio I had switched on. It occurred to me that I was the blind one, and deaf too, because I hadn't noticed him until then or realized that the radio was on.

'What song?' I asked in Malayalam, sitting up on the bench.

'The one that just got over,' Soordas said, walking into my life and sitting on a plastic chair with the white stick still in his hand. '*Eeshwarane thedithedi ponore* . . . that song.'

'Yesudas, I reckon, or Jayachandran.'

'It's from the film *Kavyamela*,' he said. 'The singer's name is Uthaman. He's from Ernakulam. Only sang five or six songs for films. He had some problems with his sight.'

'*Kavyamela*?'

'Prem Nazir acts as a blind person in it. The villain is Adoor Bhasi who steals his poems and publishes them as his own. The music is by Dakshinamoorthy.'

'Have you seen this film?' I asked a foolish question.

'I've listened to the audio track. In Kollam. My father's house is in Kollam.'

'I've met Dakshinamoorthy,' I lied. 'When I went to the Vaikom temple. He's got a flyaway beard.'

It was dark outside the shop.

'Could you switch off this light?' Soordas asked.

'Ah, so you can see a little, can't you?' I looked suspiciously at his half-closed right eye.

'No, I've been blind since birth,' he said. 'It's just that when there is light, people like you have a certain arrogance in your voice.'

I switched off the light.

'See, now we are equal,' he said.

'No, now you have the upper hand,' I said, stumbling against the bench in the dark and hurting my leg.

As soon as they got back from the holidays, the youngsters hurried into the shop.

'My hands are trembling,' one of them said as they arranged themselves around the table. 'Can't wait to play a game!'

'My *heart* is trembling,' said another. 'Last night, I fell asleep in the train and dreamt that someone was sitting behind me and eyeing my cards.'

'The song *Swapnangale, swapnangale ningal . . .* is from *Kavyamela*,' Soordas chipped in. He had been sitting unobtrusively on a bench inside the shop.

One of the youngsters turned to look at him. 'These guys have started coming here too?'

There were three blind students in their college, all of them older than the others. A room on the ground floor of the college hostel was set aside for them. The time of the day was irrelevant to them, and because of it radio music could be heard from their room at all hours, even at the hour of night when ghosts and spirits were asleep.

'Can you guys dream?' asked another young man. He was referring to the song Soordas had mentioned that described dreams as maidens from heaven.

Soordas ignored him.

'Of course they can,' I said. 'Just that they don't *see* their dreams, they hear them instead.'

'Those who are partially sighted can see dreams vaguely.'

'Vasuvannan, you won't believe me but I have seen a dream once,' Soordas said. 'Once when I was travelling in a bus from Hyderabad, I couldn't sleep for two days. When I went to bed afterwards, I saw a dream just like those with sight do. A busy road and a horse-drawn carriage . . .'

'If you don't sleep for two days, you'll go mad,' Ragesh, the most badly behaved of the youngsters, said, imitating the way Soordas walked with his white cane. 'Let's teach him to play cards. He won't see if we look at his cards, so we can beat him all the time.'

'We'll need playing cards in braille . . .'

'Braille lost his sight because of an accident with a shoe-making awl,' Soordas said. 'And when he was older, he created the braille system with the same awl.'

The youngsters looked at each other as though they were fed up with this bore. One of them sent a paper rocket flying towards his eyes. Everyone laughed, and Soordas laughed with them. I began to suspect that he had seen the rocket coming at him.

When, along with the youngsters, Soordas, too, became a regular at the shop, Selvi became angrier than usual. As it is, she was suspicious of me, her husband who, on the rare occasions when he went home to Kerala, came back a couple of weeks later than promised. She was concerned that more and more Malayalees coming into the shop might entice me back to Kerala for good.

'He doesn't even buy a biriyani,' she said, angrily squeezing tamarind into the ennai kathirikai to be served with the biriyani.

'He's not a Malayali. He's a Pattan, Tamil Brahmin. His mother is from Madras.'

'Then why do you always turn the radio to a Malayalam station as soon as he comes?'

Like most blind people, Soordas was mad about music. 'Blind people can't see anything. Pattans can't see anything beyond their own caste. So we prefer music,' Soordas explained.

'But people from your caste never made it in the movies. Yesudas is a Christian, and Brahmanandan and Kamukara are from some other castes . . .'

'Too much training is detrimental to practice, that's why. We only perform kacheri, formal concerts, and in the film world we are music directors.'

Soordas laughed loudly as though he had lost his hearing too. I smiled quietly.

'If you are laughing at my jokes, you must laugh out loud,' he said. 'Like when you're on the phone. Otherwise how will I know?'

'None of the rooms in the hostel has locks, but no one steals anything from their room,' Ragesh said, taking off his mundu and doing a dirty dance in front of Soordas. 'They don't change the fused bulbs and have set all kinds of booby traps in there for the sighted.'

'Half the time they are pretending. They can see even things that we can't see, like a woman far away.'

'The only thing worse than not being able to see is seeing what's not there,' Soordas countered.

'Slimy, these people are,' said a young man from Mannarkkad whose name I could never remember. 'Have you noticed how their wives become pregnant within the first month of their marriage?'

Everyone, including Soordas, roared with laughter.

One evening, the youngsters did not turn up, and fed up with Selvi's face and the irritating silence, Soordas and I took an autorickshaw into town. The sun had begun to set. There were only a few people at the old fort, and they looked with interest at Soordas who walked with a radio set to a high volume. Seventy years ago, such a sight would have garnered respect, and we would have been followed by a gaggle of children listening to the music. I looked at him and thought about bats who found their way by echolocation.

'I used to come here when I was young and test out ways of finding my way with sounds,' Soordas said, turning to me as though he had read my mind. 'So I never lose my way here. One time, I fell off the rock next to that entrance up there and broke my leg. That was the end of the experiments.'

Soordas walked up to the rock and sat on it as though in vengeance. 'There's some truth in what Francis said. We are greedy when it comes to women. You people can look at them but we can only see them by touch. Beauty, for you, is in your eyes, but for us it is at our fingertips.'

'Have you touched then?'

'How? Society won't let us, will it? We would need a place of complete darkness to see each other without others watching us.'

Soordas told me that he was currently in love, for the third time in his life. The two previous relationships were with women who could see. The first one left him immediately after they had a chance to be alone.

'It was my own fault,' he said. 'I was too greedy.'

'Well, you shouldn't have felt her up in such a hurry.'

We ate the crunchy snacks he had brought along in his bag and got off the rock. His second lover was very helpful, Soordas said. She wrote his exams for him and read to him. He had to fight with her to be allowed to climb a staircase by himself. She would not concede that other than not being able to see, he was perfectly able to take care of his needs.

'So I left her,' he said. 'First of all, she had an unpleasant body odour. But more importantly, she kept track of all the ways in which she was helping me as though to submit an account before God. I don't think she would have done anything to help anyone if it weren't for the Bible and Jesus Christ.'

When I met Soordas's third—and final, according to him—girlfriend, I was stunned. I was at the vegetable market discussing the rising price of onions with the vendor. From the flower market across, Soordas hooked an invisible thread on to my voice, and walked straight towards me. The mounds of banana, tomato, okra, cabbage and other produce, the coolies, the cattle grazing on the refuse, the old men picking through discarded vegetables to sell on, the customers, the lorry drivers, and the paan and lemonade stalls stared at his back as he proceeded unerringly through the crowd. The vegetable vendor's boy chucked a gooseberry into the trough left out for the cattle and water spilled silently. The woman next to him was a golden statue of some goddess gliding towards me, stunningly beautiful with voluptuous breasts and a shapely back. She did not look as though she was blind. With her wide open eyes and clear face, she looked more like an actress playing the role of a blind woman in a movie. The fragrance of the flower market followed in her wake.

'This is the Vasuvannan I told you about,' he said, introducing me to her. 'He is as mild-mannered as his voice.'

'You must have committed some horrible sin in your previous life,' I said quietly in my mind. 'You can only know a person by their voice, smell and taste. Like grabbing at a beautifully presented plate of food with your fingers in the darkness.'

'She's half Malayali,' Soordas continued. 'Not from my caste.'

'Hello,' I said mildly, touching her hand.

Soordas began to describe all the things he had in common with Vidya. They were both vegetarians, blind from birth, loved old film songs. Both had friends who took advantage of them, old scars on their left hands from using knives carelessly. Both of them liked listening to cricket commentary, curries with cauliflower, could speak Malayalam but disliked brown kuthari rice.

We went to a coffee shop and sat at a table. Flicking a piece of dosa off the table accurately, Vidya said: We were both tricked by our friends when we were young.' Her fingernails were shaped and polished, and her bangles and earrings matched the colour of her churidar top. Someone who could see was looking out for her at home, I thought.

'They would take me along to play, and then disappear quietly without telling me. I would stand there alone and cry until my parents came looking for me. Still, after a while, I was sadder if they didn't play tricks on me.'

Vidya told us that the only time she could win a game was when everyone was blindfolded. 'But even then they would cheat,' she said. 'They would say they were blindfolded and laugh at me as I tried to catch them.'

'Well, I might also trick you,' I said. Soordas listened to her laugh and laughed with her.

'We're not going home for the pooja vacation,' Ragesh said. They had moved their game to a mat spread on the floor. Illegal games like dice and cards for wagers are better played on the floor. They were planning a two-day motorbike trip to Madurai, Ramanathapuram and Dhanushkodi, and with them gone, the hostel would be empty. Without attracting their attention, I touched Soordas on his back, but he sat there motionless like a stone. Love truly made one blind and careless, and for the first time, when Soordas stepped out, his leg accidentally hit a chair.

'We could hear a "thud, thud" noise in the night around twelve,' the men said the next day. They had come earlier than usual to begin their game. 'We realized it was coming from the blind guys' room. Soordas's heart—that's what it was.'

I did not join in their laughter. When Soordas arrived in the evening, I led him to the back of the shop.

'She has agreed to come,' he said. 'She might let me kiss her, but nothing more. She doesn't have many friends so doesn't know much about these things.'

His room-mates would be gone by then. He wanted to clean the room, he said, dust it, and prise open the windowpanes stuck to the frames and let some air in. Buy an air freshener like they used in cars. The bed and mattress were infested with bedbugs, but the insecticide spray to kill them had a nasty smell.

'Just put it in the sun for a bit,' I said.

I bought a packet of high-quality condoms from the medical shop in town run by a man from Cherthala. Strawberry flavoured, it said on the packet in English.

'It's Mahanavami and you haven't laid down your weapon for pooja, Vasu,' he joked, handing me the packet hidden in his palm under the table as though he was a drug dealer selling ganja.

'It's not that,' I said, pointing to Soordas who was waiting on the other side of the road. 'I am initiating someone.'

In a deserted corner of the old fort, I took out a condom and demonstrated how to use it by putting it over Soordas's index and middle fingers.

'I doubt it will get to all this, this time,' I said. 'Still, better safe than sorry.'

Soordas tore open another one and tried it on my fingers. 'She'll chase me off if she knew what we were doing.' The tips of his fingers shook.

The hostel was as deserted and silent as a gallery after a big game. Seven of us—me, Ragesh and three other men from the card games, and two of their friends—stood waiting on the veranda of the mess hall. A handful of voices, left over from the day before, came down the stairs and quickly left the building. On the always locked door of the warden's room were obscenities in Tamil, written by the inmates. A live-in warden who had tried to bring some order to the chaos in the hostel had been beaten up by unknown assailants during a power cut. The only warden who had survived for a while was someone who was worse than the men who lived there. I warned them not to smoke or whisper. Blind people had extraordinarily sharp senses of smell and hearing, I told them. We, the sighted, only see what is in front of us. They see everything around them.

Still, at the first sight of Vidya as she approached with Soordas, one of the men made a 'ss . . . ss . . .' noise, sucking in saliva and air as though he was tasting something. The others sighed deeply, thinking about Soordas's luck as well as his misfortune. As usual, Soordas walked in front with his white stick, and Vidya followed him holding on to the left sleeve of his shirt. As I had instructed, they had left the autorickshaw two junctions before the hostel and walked the rest of the way. They were both sweating profusely. Standing on the chairs on top of the tables pulled up to all four ventilation gaps of the room, we looked into their room as they entered as though we were silent spectators of a tennis match waiting for the players to start. As though to create more darkness, Soordas shut the door and windows. A futile exercise as Ragesh had installed a bulb which now lit up the room in its milky-white brilliance. One of the young men silently took some photos on his mobile phone.

The unruly ceiling fan made listening to what was being said difficult, but I thought I heard the word 'love' filling up the room. Expressing her dissatisfaction with the cleanliness of her lover's room, she began walking around. She sniffed at the discarded clothes, found what belonged to him by smell and folded them up neatly. The air smelled of cigarettes and alcohol, she said, and complained about the suitability of his room-mates. Reminding him of the changes that would need to happen in his life, she swept the room, extracted the crumpled pieces of paper discarded under the bed and behind the table, put them in a flat cardboard box and ordered him to take it outside.

'Has she come to clean up the place?' Ragesh asked, writing on my palm with his finger. I raised my little finger, signalling patience.

Soordas took out two large chocolate bars from the jungle inside his table drawer and held it up to Vidya's nose. Happily, she sat down on the bed, and he broke off squares of the chocolate and gave them to her. When she lifted them to her lips, red as though stained by wine, Ragesh lost his control and poked me on my arm. Like an ancient sculpture, Soordas leaned over and laid his head in her lap. Her initial response was to stop him, but she relented and began combing his hair with her fingers. I began to feel that he would spend this day and night in the space between her sweet, sweet breasts and waist. He lay there and breathed in her fragrance for what seemed like the next two years or a whole lifetime, as though he was writing and rewriting a single line from a story.

'Get him! Beat him!'

Without waiting for my signal, Ragesh shouted, and in the next second, he and his friends kicked open the boltless door and entered the room.

'Doing the dirty in the hostel when there is no one else around!'

They slapped Soordas across the face and kicked him to the floor. A lone spectator in the gallery, I stood where I was and watched the game unfold through the ventilation gap. One of them slapped Vidya's cheek, caught her by her hair and banged her head against the wall, while another, like a child who had been given a birthday cake, grabbed her breasts and buttocks. I checked my watch, and when exactly six minutes had passed, I ran into the room panting as though I had run a marathon.

'Stop!' I shouted at the young men attacking her. 'Leave the poor girl alone!'

Then I 'rescued' her from her attackers by grabbing her hand and running out of the room.

I sat her behind me on my scooter and took her into town. 'What foolishness he did!' I said, hailing an autorickshaw. 'A man bringing a young woman to a hostel in broad daylight!'

'He said there would be no one there,' Vidya said. 'He said Vasuvannan said it would be all right.'

'He said that? He really shouldn't have done this to you.'

Fear filled her face. Slipping her feet into the sandals I had bought her to replace the pair she had lost in the hostel room, she got into the autorickshaw. I supported her as she stumbled and pushed her inside.

'Now I'll tell you a story.'

I held my lips close to her ear so that my voice would not drown in the noise of the bus. It had turned north past two districts and past Madurai, past coconut groves and cultivated land, and now travelled through a scrubby landscape. Two weeks had passed, and the shock of the incident had almost left her. I was considering at which unknown place we should get off the bus.

'Once upon a time, there was a very beautiful blind girl,' I continued. 'A man was deeply in love with her.

'"Will you marry me?" he asked her, for the hundredth time.

'"Not now," she said, for the hundredth time. "I'll marry only when I am able to see."

'One day the man told her: "Someone has promised to donate their eyes to you."

'This made her very happy. And before long, the operation was done, and she was able to open her eyes and see the world for the first time.

'"Let's get married now," he said.

'"How can I who can see marry you who are blind?" she asked him. "You must find someone suitable for yourself." And then, in a gruffer voice, she said: "We won't see each other again."

'Deeply hurt, he watched her walk away from him mercilessly. "My dearest," he called out in a frayed voice. "Please take good care of my eyes."'

Vidya gripped my hand. Tears flowed out of her eyes used only to cry.

'Vasuvannan, where are we going?' she asked me.

'That's not my name,' I said. 'I am a storyteller.'

'What's this on your fingers?' She raised my fingers to her nose. 'Oh, the ink from your pen,' she answered her own question. 'Seems it's all over your hand.'

I pulled my hand away, and surreptitiously wiped the redness of guilt off my fingers.

alone

Ahaha! How sad to think there is, in this world,
Nothing more wretched than human existence

—Kumaranasan, *Karuna*

'Aren't you getting off?'

Desperately hanging on to the ticket rack with his left hand, the conductor, who looked neither young nor old, asked him. 'The place you bought the ticket for is far behind us.'

'Yes! Stop the bus!' he said, waking up suddenly and looking anxiously into the night. Whether the conductor rang the bell or not or the driver stopped the bus or not, he found himself in the darkness outside as the bus sped away towards its destination.

Later, he would re-examine those unclear moments several times in his mind. Were there other passengers in the bus? And were they, except, perhaps, for a handful, asleep, swinging like damaged pendulums? Did a couple of them wake up at the sound of the conductor's voice and look at him with interest? Perhaps a child had laughed.

He thought the conductor had grabbed his shoulder and shaken him awake. The leftover pain in his shoulder must be from the conductor's fingers. Or did he bang it against something when he scrambled up? He tried to imagine that the conductor had, with the help of some passengers, pushed him out of the bus. In the end, he decided that, in the anxiety of having missed his stop, he had got out by himself.

The congealed darkness knocked against his leg and hurt him. In the silence, the sound of the bus engine still reverberated in his ears. As his sleep-addled mind cleared and the feeling of anxiety left him, he began to doubt whether he had even been in a bus. All he was sure of was the fact that he was here, on this road, in the dark. He shook off such muddled thoughts with a smile.

As his eyes adjusted to the darkness, he realized the place was completely deserted. He had acted foolishly. He should have bought another ticket and remained in the bus until he could get off at a proper stop with at least a couple of shops. Reluctant to believe his complete isolation, he looked around in the hope of seeing a faraway light from a house yet to retire for the night. But there was nothing except for a light breeze.

As always, the four of them—Kunjumon, Devasia, Punnan and Soman—had got on the bus and sat together in the long back seat. He was never alone in the bus because he was not the one who got out last. They would sit together chatting and laughing, his jokes always drawing the most laughs. He was known for his jokes at their workplace too. He would make up salacious stories about Beena, who had big breasts and a round behind, and Soman, stories that sounded almost real and sent everyone into a cacophony of laughter. And when his stories threatened to completely cross the boundary of decency, Soman would scold him, but his reluctant use of swear words would make them laugh even more. He always got off at his stop, leaving them a nugget to laugh about.

He stood by the side of the road for a long while, hoping for the headlights of a bus or a private vehicle. The area was flat, and the road went off into the distance without any bends. Thinking that the vehicles speeding through the deserted night might have enough time to see him and stop, he walked into the middle of the road and stood there. Until a moment ago, he knew clearly the direction he had come from, but now he had lost track of which way he was headed. If he had to go right, he should be standing to the left of the road, and vice versa.

A sudden sound froze him in his tracks. Perhaps a snake or a rat moving in the dry leaves. He stepped off the tarmac and realized there were no dry leaves on the verges, not even dry stalks of grass. His inchoate fear scared him. One's mind might pretend to be happy or sad, but fear is different. He was not the type of person who panicked and made a ruckus upon seeing a snake. Wondering why he was feeling scared, the traveller walked carefully forward. He didn't have to be scared of darkness or of ghosts, or even of thieves or robbers who might be skulking around like spirits. All he had in his possession was his lunch box that was not even washed properly, and a small amount of money.

Usually, he paid no attention to small noises, but when there was another disturbance, his ears pricked up. At first, it sounded like water flowing in a small canal but he realized it was the sound made by winged termites swarming out of the soil. He thrust his hand into the swarm. If he hadn't fallen asleep in the bus and ended up unexpectedly at this deserted place, a few more termites would have staggered into the sky instead of hitting his hand and falling back on to the soil. He surmised, wrongly, that there were houses nearby, and that their owners had switched off the lights against the swarming insects.

At that moment, he came very close to figuring out the reason for his fear. It was the first time he was so completely alone. 'I've never seen anyone who refuses to be alone even when he goes to the toilet, and continues to talk to someone outside,' his wife had exclaimed soon after they were married.

'I was not alone even in my mother's womb,' he had replied. 'And when we came out, we had all these brothers and sisters waiting for us.'

In the mornings, when he and his siblings would form a line and walk to the northern compound to defecate, children in the neighbourhood who had no siblings would call out, somewhat dejected: 'There goes the shitters' procession.'

They would sit in a row and shit until the place was called shit yard. In the nights, they would sleep, pushing and kicking one another, on two mats on the floor.

As a strapping young man, when he first got a job at the company, he had tried to get a woman to fall in love with him. After the siren announcing the end of the workday, accompanied by seven or eight of his friends, he would follow her home, trying, along the way, to get her to talk to him. 'What's the point in even considering it?' she asked those who intervened on his behalf. 'He is never alone!'

As he stood with his back to the road, he felt that a vehicle passed him by, and that the lightless, soundless, exhaustless vehicle had travelled through his mind. He should have put his arm out and it might have stopped. It could have been his last chance to escape the night's gelatinous darkness. He imagined that he felt the wind as the soundless vehicle passed by him, and that the leaves of the few sparse plants trembled in it.

In that state, he looked into himself and talked, somewhat loudly. Just some random prattle, just loud enough to hear if a dozen people were standing around. He had seen old-timers at the beginning of mental imbalance talk like this, gesticulating. With an innate sense of embarrassment, he looked around to see if anyone had seen him, and walked on. In the feeling of complete freedom, he hitched up his mundu and scratched his butt, and released a loud fart.

'Even that nasty bastard would do,' he said, kicking the earth, thinking about an old man he and his friends had once beaten to a pulp. He had forgotten the reason for it, except that the old man had done something wrong, something like trying to hurt a child he had been left alone with.

'I would explain myself if you were alone,' the old man had told him when he had bashed his face in. That night, he had gone to bed thinking that his blows were not strong enough as he had no previous experience in beating up people. And he had dreamt something about his arms and legs not following where his mind went. He rarely had dreams because he was in the habit of talking through most of the night, falling asleep late and waking up early. If he could find the old man now, he could have sat across from him and listened to his rationalizations.

Presently, he noticed that he was walking on a lane of packed, dry dust that had branched off the main road. It looked like it was about to rain, and if it did, he could experience that unique, earthy smell for the first time. A small building stood jutting into the lane, and when he saw it, he felt as happy as though he had run into a person. It looked like a shop, just a room and a veranda. He ran his hand over the low wall surrounding the veranda, examined it and sat down. The dust had been wiped off by those who had sat there during the day. Discarded pieces of paper crunched under his feet.

He could read the big letters written on the walls even in the darkness. ____ Memorial Reading Room. The letters spelling out in whose memory it had been set up had faded away. Must be Indira Gandhi Memorial Reading Room, he thought.

'She was a woman with balls,' he had said to his wife on the day Indira Gandhi died. His children were named Rajeev and Sanjay. He had never come across reading rooms named after them. Probably because he hadn't really paid attention—one only sees what one is interested in.

It did not surprise him to register that he had never read anything other than his schoolbooks and newspapers. He only read the headlines in the newspapers and avoided the rest, saying that things had not changed since his birth.

Even the day before, looking at a man sitting in the corner of the canteen with his head buried in a book, he had joked with his friends: 'Look, what I used to say has come true. Earlier, if you walked around with a thick book in your hand, people would look at you with respect. These days they think there's something wrong with you.'

The door to the building was old-fashioned—a series of wooden planks that could be raised up. He gave it a shake, testing its strength. He paced the short veranda, anxiously thinking about his wife and children. Worried that he had not returned from work, would she, by now, have raised a ruckus and alerted the neighbours? Or would she have gone peacefully to sleep, assuming that he had decided to work a second shift? He felt bad that his children would be happy in his absence, relieved that he wasn't there to threaten them and make them do their homework. He had come to know that they were happier when he was not around, and had been giving some thought to changing his strict ways.

He gave the door to the reading room another shake. Peeping into the darkness through a gap in the planks, he marvelled at the stories and poems that must be inside. Suddenly, a pleasant thought came to him. What if someone—a bookworm—was still inside, reading in the light of a candle? What if there was a mountain of books that he had read piled up to his left, and an even bigger pile of yet-to-read books to his right? What if, worried about his advancing age and depleting eyesight, this man was reading the books with a great sense of urgency? He banged on the door, calling out, 'Is anyone there? Is anyone there?' If he had a crowbar, he would have prised the door open, and rubbing a couple of stones together like the cavemen, he would have made light and read at least one book.

Dejected, he sat back on the wall of the veranda and tried to recall his schoolbooks. He came up with nothing. Even in the heat, a pale mist floated in and covered him. He sat silently with his eyes closed, and to his surprise, he remembered a couple of lines of poetry.

Atha vilangunnu bhavadganangalaal
Swathe chuzhannee panineer malarchedi

'See how glorious the rose, already beautiful, with the fireflies on her.' Lines that some poet wrote to entertain children. He rarely remembered things from the past, even the names of his friends. He leaned against the pillar. Still anxious, he adjusted his position and closed his eyes.

Was it a minute or a century before he opened his eyes? He tried to lie down on the veranda, but worried that his body was getting sticky with sweat, he sat up again. Hoping for a sliver of breeze, he stepped out and walked around, sometimes dejected and sometimes energetic, turning round and round in circles to his right and to his left. By now, he had lost all sense of direction.

He did not know any more where the lane and the veranda he had rested upon were, and this fact gave him a mild sense of happiness. There was no use worrying any more. Deciding that the right side of his body faced east, he turned around slowly and walked to the south that he had just created for himself.

The sky above, studded with brilliant stars, was an upturned basket, and he lay down on the bare earth below it. Watching the basket, woven with the leaves of the screw pine, he thought about an old friend. He and his friends had once lain under the open sky like this, at midnight, while making their raucous way back from a festival.

'Halley's Comet will appear here tonight,' his friend had told them, gravely watching the sky. 'They said so in *Eureka*. Happens only once every seventy-six years.'

But when he saw that his mates were about to pee on him, the skygazer rolled away.

'This will take seventy-six years to reach the bottom,' said his friends as they peed into the deep, unused well nearby.

It dawned on him that he had not seen even a rainbow, having spent all his life looking only down at the earth like a pig. He had almost seen one when he had taken his family on a company excursion. When the dam's shutters were opened, the water spray in the morning sun had made a small rainbow, but he and his friends were off searching for an arrack shop. And by the time the excursion party reached Shanghumugham, he was so drunk that he had missed seeing the sea.

'Papa, lick my hand,' his son told him that night. 'It's salty from the sea.'

His house was only thirty kilometres away from the sea, but he had never felt the need to go and look at it.

As an endless sea surging in the darkness took shape inside him, he scrambled up. It did not matter if the sea was three thousand kilometres away. He would get there, walk all the way there. He set out at a brisk pace towards the west he had created for himself, and as he walked, he learnt to play a secret game with his mind. Focus on what it is that you are thinking about right now, and when you are certain that focusing on what you are thinking is your current thought, focus on it with a secretive smile and wait for further thoughts to develop. He walked, at a fair clip, through the long corridor created by two mirrors facing each other.

Noticing a luminescence in the distance, he walked towards it, and realized it was a swarm of fireflies flying close to the ground. Some rested on a plant and shone like the lost crown of a king in some story. He picked a leaf off the plant, squeezed it between his fingers and smelled it, and recognized it as a thumba plant. The fireflies took flight with the arrival of the human. He ran after them and caught one with great difficulty and held it inside his fist. His hand glittered as though he had a diamond ring on his finger.

And then a scary thought passed through his mind calmly. What if, in other places, the sun had risen several times? What if this place would never again see the light of day? What if eons had gone by since his wife and children had stopped crying for him?

lord of the hunt

To him, it felt as though a majestic lion had sauntered into the cool, clean room, and taking the computer screen to be the trunk of an ungu tree, rubbed its face against it. But which of the two men was the lion? One was middle-aged, dressed in a saffron mundu and a khaki shirt, and sported a pointy moustache. The other, clean-shaven and dressed in a pair of trousers, was quite young. The moustached man had a plastic bag printed with the name of a textile shop in Kumali in his hand. Droplets of blood fell on the clean, white floor tiles like the bright-red seeds of a manjaadi tree.

'Dileepan sir?' the clean-shaven man asked in a respectful voice.

Dileepan lunged forward and grabbed the plastic bag.

'Two parcels of two kilo each, sir,' the man continued. 'Twelve hundred rupees, altogether.'

Dileepan carried the plastic bag into the room set aside for the staff to eat their lunch and read their newspapers. He called two of his friends, people he looked upon with a great deal of respect, on the phone.

'I have wild game, about a kilo,' he said. 'Do you want some?'

It was evident from his breathing that, for the first time in their relationship, he had the upper hand.

'Tell you what. I'll cook it myself and bring it over. You organize a bottle of something to drink.'

He then went to Gracykutty, the most attractive of all the clerks at the bank, and brought her quietly into the room. Wrapping up some meat, he put it in a separate bag and gave it to her.

'Oh, you shouldn't have bothered,' she said politely.

'No, no, take it,' he said. 'You don't need to pay for it.'

Just then, Ramachandra Hedgan entered the room. 'Dileepan, aren't you an assistant manager?' he asked.

'Yes, sir.'

'Look at all these flies in your room!'

It was only when he was speeding home on his scooter, having taken the rest of the day off, that Dileepan remembered he had forgotten to wash the bloodstains off his hand. And there in front of him, near the traffic lights, right in the middle of a sea of vehicles, was a blue Maruti car. The moustached man sat in the back seat. The clean-shaven one was driving the car, and beside him sat a suspicious-looking young woman. Dileepan waved at them but they did not see him. Suddenly, two incidents that could happen in the next few days came to him.

One: Lunch hour at the bank where everyone sat together with their overfilled lunch boxes bursting forth like excited children.

'These days you always have wild game meat,' Minimol, who was famous for her fried clams, says. 'What happened to your usual drumsticks and beans and aubergines?'

'Come on, madam, you say that because you don't know the value of drumsticks,' Babukuttan's innuendo makes everyone laugh.

Two: A headline in the next day's newspaper. 'Bank employee arrested for possession of illegal sambar deer meat.' Accompanying the headline is his photograph in which he is dressed only in his underpants and is standing next to a plastic bag with his arms crossed.

Dileepan imagined surrendering to the police. It occurred to him that there was something honourable in such a picture, like a magician burning to death while completing a fire-escape trick, something people marvelled at, that set them wondering jealously why he had attempted such a feat.

Dr Prasannan sampled the meat. 'Eating wild game is like the doctor having an affair with one of the nurses,' he said, chewing on a piece. 'It's forbidden, and so you don't want anyone knowing about it, but really you want the whole world to find out.'

They had been friends since Dileepan had been transferred to the local branch of the bank. Dileepan did not join their drinking sessions often, and the doctor regarded him with a bit of contempt because of it. Dileepan drank only beer, and that too in moderate amounts. The doctor liked acting out, for the entertainment of his drinking buddies, a fake story about how Dileepan got senselessly drunk after only a glass of beer.

'I don't think there is any man who doesn't want the whole world to know that he has partaken in poached meat,' Shaji, the doctor's manservant, said.

Dileepan looked admiringly at him, a man who spent his entire life in the kitchens of prominent men, and laughed loudly in a self-congratulatory manner.

'Drinking arrack, playing cards and hunting. These are the real signs of masculinity,' Shaji continued, making them laugh uproariously again.

'I went hunting once,' Dileepan said. 'When I was quite young . . .'

'What for, to catch flies?' the doctor asked, looking at him with distaste. The front of his shirt was stained with bits of meat and meat juice. He poured the gravy into his glass and drank it in one gulp, and then began licking it clean with his finger. 'Sambar this is not. A muntjac, most likely.'

Ignoring Dileepan's protests, Shaji supported the doctor. 'There isn't even a dozen sambar deer in the High Range!' he said disdainfully.

Later, Dileepan stood in front of a government official who regarded him with the same disdain. He was submitting an application for a gun licence.

'Licences are given if the gun is for the protection of crops,' the official informed him. 'How many hectares of land do you have?'

'I am living in a rented house here . . .'

'Your permanent address is in Idukki. How much land do you have there?'

'Ten cents.'

'Must have got it because of the Land Reform Act, right?' The man looked at Dileepan and gave him a condescending smile.

Still, Dileepan managed to procure the licence after pleading with the official that it was his long-standing desire to own a gun, and reminding him of the many personal loans the bank sanctioned for government employees. When he stepped out of the office, he imagined he had caught a porcupine in a trap.

The phone rang, and the voice at the other end told him that they would deliver some wild boar meat by noon. He had been pestering them with calls for a few days now, and the man said it was the first time the same person had made so many calls.

'It's like you are desperate for some life-saving medicine. Like you've become addicted to the taste of wild meat . . .'

'It's not the taste of the meat itself,' Dileepan said. 'It's the taste behind the meat . . .'

'Not sure what you mean, sir . . .' The man sounded baffled.

Dileepan had met him for the first time when he had come to the bank looking for an agricultural loan.

Dileepan was back at the bank in fifteen minutes. Instead of waiting for the lift, he ran quickly up the stairs and went to his colleagues, and made a list of their orders. Two kilos for Gracykutty, one for Babukuttan . . . When he got to Hedgan, he looked distastefully at Dileepan.

'Aren't you an assistant manager?' he asked again. 'When I look at you, I am reminded of a large piece of meat hanging off a hook in a butcher shop.'

Dileepan told him that he was taking the day off and left without waiting for a response. Outside, he bought a sherbet, and as he stood there drinking it and waiting for the men, he imagined the conversation upstairs in the bank:

'It's as though someone has been putting kaivisham, black magic, in Dileepan's wild meat,' Minimol says.

'Remember that time we went to Gavi on a day trip?' Gracykutty asks. 'It was like he went berserk when he saw the forest. Went knowingly down the elephant trail deep into the forest and didn't come out till it was dark. There were king cobras there!'

'He knows the names of all the trees and plants in the forest. And even the slightest movement in the bushes gets him excited.'

'All the same,' Hedgan chips in, looking wide-eyed at them, 'he is quite diligent in his duties.'

When the men arrived, Dileepan tried to persuade them to go to a bar.

'No, sir,' the clean-shaven man—his name was Ajeesh—said. 'That would be risky.'

He was alert and vigilant as though he was still in the forest, thought Dileepan with a sense of respect for the man. After a short, low-voiced argument, they bought a bottle of rum and got in the car.

'I have a request,' Dileepan said, carefully pouring the rum into plastic glasses as the car jolted along the potholes in the road. 'Don't bother selling to those ignoramuses who eat wild game and say it tastes like beef.'

Kurian, the moustached man, pulled the car to the side of the road. 'That's true, sir,' he said, laughing. 'To be honest, wild meat is not all that special, but no one will admit it. They eat it with the same satisfaction as though they have personally gone to the forest and killed the animal.'

'But that's the thing, Kurian,' Dileepan said. 'One must remember the forest when eating wild game, the darkness and the cold, and the hunter's eyes . . .'

He was about to ask them whether he could join them for a hunt when Ajeesh spotted a police jeep on the road.

'We must be careful,' he said.

'Tell them to get lost! If hunting is a crime, then eating is a crime too.' Dileepan was angry. 'Have you read the stories of Kapish?' he asked Ajeesh.

'Of course!' Ajeesh smiled, thinking of the monkey in the popular children's comic series. 'There's a hunter in it, Doppayya.'

'I feel great sympathy for the man. He's not been able to catch even a pangolin so far. Kapish won't let him.'

'Next time I'm going to get Kapish,' Kurian said, starting the car and stepping on the accelerator.

'I saw a woman with you in the car the other day . . .'

'Yes, we picked her up to avoid police checking. We spend all the money we make from this on women and drinks. We don't take it home.'

'Well, it is money cursed by poor voiceless creatures, after all,' Dileepan joked.

The car heated up like a rock in the summer sun. Even the sparse grass at the verges was dry despite the slight rain of the previous night. A lone rabbit wandered into the grass, licked its mouth and disappeared again. Dileepan inhaled the aroma of blood mixed with turmeric powder. The meat parcels were liberally sprinkled with the stuff to avoid detection by sharp-nosed forest guards. The edges of Dileepan's trousers were soaked in the blood that had leaked and pooled under the seat.

'This is a forest with no undergrowth,' Kurian said as the car entered a rich neighbourhood. 'Like in the comics, all neatly laid out with animals that speak and monkeys that wear clothes. Some even have magic powers.' He pulled up in front of a house where a man was waiting for them. 'And here we have a bear,' he said.

As Kurian handed over a parcel, Dileepan watched the expression on the man's face, reverential as though he was turning the pages of a children's book. He imagined Kurian drawing a double-barrelled gun from the air and shooting down the bear. The bear falls, only to come alive again in the next story.

Soon, it was dark. They abandoned the car and went into the deep forest on horseback. They stood silently by the side of a hill watching the shola forest frozen in the moonlight. A low growl emerged, agitating the horses, and they charged into the forest holding aloft their swords and spears. Dileepan wished those who knew him could see him then. He was always in front of an invisible, imagined, female spectator.

In the night, Dileepan's wife sat next to him as though he was a pitiable villain. 'Yesterday Cecily asked me whether my husband has started a side business of selling wild meat,' she said. 'You and your friends have been to her house three times in two months, she said.'

'Well, that woman is the type who says Taj Mahal is a cemetery,' he retorted angrily.

'I told her that you were an animal lover. That time when you saw a rabbit being killed . . . You cried, remember?'

'I don't remember,' Dileepan said, embarrassed.

'I don't forget anything,' his wife continued without sparing any of the details. 'Once you paid a lot of money and bought a dried-up head of a wild buffalo. And you nagged me to give our firstborn the strange name "Jim Corbett".'

Annoyed, he got up and began playing with his children.

'I'm a fierce, man-eating tiger,' he said.

'Bang! Bang! Bang . . . !' They shot him down.

Early the next morning, Dileepan took the bus, almost empty because it was a holiday, and travelled east. He placed the long package in his hand on the luggage rack above, and sat a few seats away, watching whether his fellow passengers were showing signs of curiosity. He had used up more than a month's salary to secretly procure the locally made gun. By the time the sun was warm, the bus stopped at a junction—a depression where three hillsides met—with only a couple of shops. From there, he took a jeep, and after a couple of hours of travel, it left him at a footpath where he began his ascent into the forest.

He walked steadily on, stopping to pick a leaf and smell it, and listen to the call of the giant forest squirrel. As he climbed up a steep incline effortlessly, a little girl playing in the yard of a small house below a rocky outcrop looked up and smiled at him. In the old days, the only person that the woman of the house entertained was the hunter Uppayi. He wondered how the little girl was related to them.

Farther up, he came to the one-room house made of cement blocks. An elderly woman sat in the yard searching for something.

'Thalle . . .' He called her 'old woman' in his usual unsympathetic, leathery voice.

'Did you bring anything?' she asked, spitting out the chewing tobacco in her mouth. Happily, she grabbed the half bottle of cheap rum he had brought.

'You've become fat!' she said. 'Like an ash gourd.'

He lifted the lids of a couple of pots in the room and peered in. 'Haven't you been catching and eating rats, thalle?'

'Didn't you say your whore of a wife was ashamed of it? So I stopped.'

After eating the kanji and mashed colocasia, he went eagerly to the back of the house. In the scant space behind the house stood a lonely murikku tree with fire-red flowers, and beyond that, the barrier put up by forest guards. He raised his gun and fired two shots into the forest beyond. A family of mongoose scampered away in the undergrowth. He imagined he was posing for a photograph with a smoking gun after having shot down a fearsome tiger, and that, after his death, his children would frame the photograph and hang it reverentially on the wall of his house.

maoist

Early in the morning of the day after the police knocked on Prabhakaran's door asking questions about a bloodied poster that had appeared on the library wall and about a couple of stick-thin strangers from the forest who had turned up at a nearby house begging for rice, there was another knock.

'Aiyo! Told you yesterday itself, didn't I?' Prabhakaran said, trembling. The lingering buzz of the alcohol he had imbibed the previous night escaped through the open window like the last breath from a dying body. 'I'm not a Naxalite, never been one. I swear I don't know Ajitha or Venu.'

He had good reason to be scared of the police. During 1980–85, Prabhakaran had spent his days sitting on the culvert near the chapel, convinced that a postman with magic powers would bring him an appointment letter for a government job he had not even applied for. In that time, his beard and hair grew so long that he looked like a revolutionary from 1970–75. And when people with the means to eat four square meals a day began looking at him suspiciously, he had an idea. He bought a postcard and sent an anonymous letter to Kuriachan, a local dignitary and one of the first people to establish a rubber plantation in the area. The letter said: 'Leave five one-hundred rupee notes on the eastern wall of the church, and weigh it down with a small stone. Do this by 5 p.m. tomorrow or else! Naxalbari Zindabad.' The very next evening, the police picked him up, sat him on the floor of their jeep, took him to the station and locked him up. Someone got him released from custody, but when he came out, his hair was cropped and his face was clean-shaven. From that day on, he began to talk in a measured and calculated manner, and people began to pay attention to what he had to say.

The knocking became louder and insistent, and finally Prabhakaran opened the door. In the fragile darkness giving way to a new day, stood Kaalan Varky, the local butcher. Sweat dripped off his body, and he looked very worried. A stench of stale tobacco from his uncleaned teeth combined with that of blood, soaked into his hands from the age of fifteen, emanated from him.

'Come out and help, Prabhakara,' Varky said, panting. 'Call everyone. The buffaloes—the male and the female—to be butchered tomorrow have escaped! They're running around all over the place. Come, quick!'

'I am coming,' Prabhakaran said. 'After all, this is the land that worships a buffalo-slayer as god,' he added philosophically.

'Which god is that?'

'Ayyappan. Sabarimala Ayyappan.'

'That bull-buffalo came all the way from Andhra.'

'Aiyo! Was it from Telangana? If so, he'll definitely cause some damage,' said Prabhakaran.

He meant it as a joke, but it was indeed the truth. The buffalo had learnt to skip and skitter by the fourth day of his birth. As he was entertaining himself, butting his head against the haystack, his master, Jogayya, who had just returned from the day's labour in the bajra field, approached him quietly with a piece of cloth and a rope in his hand. Jogayya's plan was to overpower the young calf and suffocate him to death with the cloth. It was what they did—what they had always done—in those parts. Bull calves were not allowed to live longer than a week because they drank up all the milk of the mother buffalo, and sent the owner into penury. The custom was to kill the bull calves, skin them, stuff the skin with straw and stick it on an iron rod, which would fool the mother buffalo into releasing plentiful milk thinking it was her son until, a few days later, she would forget all about him and keep on giving milk anyway.

On the day Jogayya was getting ready to kill the bull calf, his son Bhanu was home from college on a week's break. As his father approached the calf, Bhanu looked up from the book he was reading. 'Let him be, Appa,' he said. 'Don't kill him.'

Jogayya looked at his son. Twenty years old and of no particular use to anyone, and always with his head in a book. He muttered something lovingly and walked away. The day after the young man went back to college, Jogayya returned from the field, and forgetting that his son had already left, called out: 'Bhanu . . .' The bull calf came bounding up to him. Jogayya looked at him curiously, scratched his head and petted him. From then on, Jogayya and his wife called him 'Bhanu' and fed him lovingly and lavishly. Even after the mother buffalo's udders dried up and eventually she died, the fattened bull calf frolicked unfettered across the fields and the farmyard.

Exactly two years later, a green-painted jeep rode around the village asking for Jogayya and finally arrived in his compound. Assuming they were people from the bank come to demand the repayment of the loan, Jogayya's wife began wailing while he stood bowing apologetically.

'Where's your son?' asked a stocky man in a black shirt and dark sunglasses.

'He's studying, sir. In Delhi. Not working yet . . .'

'He'll make work for us,' the man said. He caught Jogayya by the fastening of his lower garments and squeezed his loins. 'Tell that scoundrel to come to the police station.'

The next market day, Jogayya tied a rope around Bhanu's neck and took him to the auction.

'Don't sell him to butchers,' he whispered in the auctioneer's ear. 'There might be someone who would want to raise him?'

It was 4 a.m. The market was buzzing with people with banknotes stuffed in their waistbands, vendors selling black tea, lorry drivers and cattle. Money exchanged hands in the faint light, and people held the notes up to the dim bulbs and flickering lamps, examining them suspiciously.

'For sure . . .' said the auctioneer.

Cattle buyers stood around the plump and gleaming Bhanu, enthusiastically making bids. As the sun rose, Bhanu walked up a ramp into a large truck along with tired, old cart oxen and elderly buffaloes. Two or three hours later, the truck stopped at another market and loaded up another bunch of animals. Among them was a female buffalo, younger and with a more supple and gleaming body than Bhanu.

'You have your work cut out,' the driver told Bhanu, smirking suggestively as he poked a stick up the cow-buffalo's anus and manhandled her into the truck. 'The two of you can make out until you get there.'

Kaalan Varky walked hurriedly with Prabhakaran to the spot from where the buffaloes had broken free. 'Ran off just now, the two of them!' he said. 'One to the east and the other to the south.' They had no specific plan in mind to catch the beasts. Prabhakaran had, for no particular reason, brought the cane he used to scare his children. And as is ubiquitous in crisis situations, he had wrapped a cotton towel around his head.

Varky unleashed a chain of swear words and declared that the two animals were in heat. 'Not one buffalo has escaped from me till today. Now see, two of them together! The bull got loose first. As he was running away, the cow-buffalo bayed, and he came right back and got her off her tether with his horns.'

Amazed, Prabhakaran gaped at him.

'You could have stopped him, Varkicha, couldn't you?' he asked stupidly, and was rewarded with another obscene word from Varky.

'Who can stop a raging buffalo? Your father? I thrashed him good on his hump but he hooked me with his horns and tossed me aside. See . . .' Varky showed Prabhakaran the scrapes on his legs and arms.

'Where was Anthony?'

'Don't talk to me about that darling son of a bitch. One rain and he disappears for two days. Must be on some canal bank with his fishing net.'

Varky had barely finished when Anthony ran up a short, steep lane, and stood before them. Two lengths of tether ropes were coiled around his arm. Varky gave him an earful as though Anthony had personally untied the buffaloes and let them loose. Anthony's shins and feet were covered in gloopy mud as though he had just stepped out of a canal. Blood trickled from a small wound below a knee, caused perhaps by a sharp stone or a thorn, but he seemed unconcerned about it. Another bellow from Varky sent him running eastwards looking for signs of the buffalo. Producing a strange siren-like sound from deep within their throats, Varky and Prabhakaran ran southwards.

Having been expelled from home by his father, Anthony had grown up eating jackfruits and mangoes that were plentiful from the month of Kumbham, and doing odd jobs here and there when the season was over. He had started working as a helper in Kaalan Varky's butcher shop five or six years ago. One busy Sunday, when Anthony came to buy the potti—bones and knuckles for the toddy shop—Varky put him to work chopping the meat. After that, Anthony presented himself at the butcher shop at 3 a.m. every morning to help with the day's slaughter. When the sun rose and the man from the chai shop brought them their breakfast—kallappam and egg curry—he ate it without wiping the blood off his fingers. When the cook from the vicarage or other local dignitaries came to the shop, Varky would cut a large chunk of prime meat, trim off the fat and sinew, and chuck it towards Anthony, who would dice it with a sharp knife into neat little pieces that could almost be eaten raw, pack it in plastic bags and deliver it to their vehicles. The portions sent to the convent and the toddy shop were 'seconds' mixed with fat, tongue and other offal. Anthony set upon them somewhat cruelly, hacking them mercilessly on the wooden chopping block, careless about the shape or the size of the bits. By 11 a.m., when the work quietened somewhat, he would set out on a bicycle with several portions of meat wrapped in teak leaves. These were to be delivered to the houses of a few Nairs and Ambalavasis who, for some unknowable reason, considered going to the butcher shop to buy their own meat beneath their dignity. Varky routinely took advantage of their lack of experience in telling good-quality meat from the inferior. Mindful of their wishes, Anthony would avoid the front entrance of their properties, and go in through the back to the pot placed on the kitchen step, and deposit the meat parcels surreptitiously in them. At that moment, long, lustful sighs would escape from the houses in anticipation of the fragrance that would emanate as the meat cooked in a watery gravy of onions, coconut milk and spices.

Back at the shop, Anthony's weekly exertions would end only when he had dropped the moon-white bones stripped of meat into the waterhole to decay, buried the innards and other useless bits, thoroughly scrubbed the floor of the shop with coconut husk and soap as though getting rid of evidence of a murder, and sprinkled it with lemongrass oil. By then, sitting on a plastic chair out in the yard in front of the shop, Kaalan Varky would be halfway through a bottle of arrack. Cursing out Anthony's long-dead mother and the pigs he reared lovingly on special feed, rooting around near the septic tanks, he would occasionally share a glass with Anthony.

No one knew which animal had run east and which to the south. By the time Varky organized a bunch of people, a terrible accident had taken place at the junction. The bundles of newspapers that should have reached homes in the early morning and two cylinders of milk that should, by then, have been at the milk society, lay strewn and spilled on the road. The confused milkman and the newspaper man, their bicycles broken and blood trickling from their elbows, described what had happened to the assembled crowd. At the sight of the charging buffalo, they had lost control of their bicycles and run headlong into each other, but they declared, in a unified voice, that he had tossed them aside with his horns.

'We were standing over there, see, out of the way, but he came right at us and gored us,' the milkman said.

'It wasn't the bull, it was the cow,' the other man disagreed. 'A rampaging bull-buffalo is more dangerous than an elephant.'

The crowd's combined accusatory look generated another volley of obscenities from Varky, and he ran in the direction the buffalo had taken off. Raman, an erstwhile footballer whose job now was to bring the post from the nearby town, joined the chasers armed with a sickle.

'Don't you have to go get the post?' Prabhakaran asked, panting.

'How can I go when these two are loose? I'll go tomorrow.'

'Oh, what a remarkable buffalo!' Prabhakaran exclaimed. 'Ten minutes untethered and he has put paid to milk, newspaper and the post!'

They stopped at a house and looked suspiciously at the broken fence posts in front of it. The house belonged to Paul, a former Congress party activist who was now a farmer. Ignoring his lungs, overused and damaged by years of smoking, Kaalan Varky ran up the steps and knocked loudly on the front door. Paul opened the door immediately as though he had been waiting behind it. With his desiccated body that remained fatless even in advanced age, he looked like M.A. John, the veteran Congress leader.

'Which way did he go, Paul?' Varky asked him.

'Why are you running after him, Varkicha? Let him go live in a forest,' Paul said philosophically, folding his lungi up and stepping out. 'Leave him in peace. He'll live somewhere without troubling anyone.'

He had barely finished speaking when they saw an amazing sight. The bull-buffalo jumped off the low stone stile of the adjacent compound, and ran, in a cloud of dust, into the yard right below where they stood. As soon as he saw them, he turned back and ran into a compound farther away next to a quarry. Confused, he trampled back and forth a couple of times. In less than a minute, almost fifty banana trees of the etha variety and around ten trellises of beans and paaval—crop that

Paul had nurtured without even a touch of chemicals or pesticides, feeding them only cow dung, wood ash and jeevamrutham, a liquid fertilizer involving cow urine—lay destroyed on the trodden earth. Calling out an obscene word that put Kaalan Varky to shame, Paul grabbed whatever he could to use as a weapon and ran after the animal with murderous intent. Despite the grey hair on his chest, he had the energy of an eighteen-year-old from a disciplined lifestyle and nature-friendly food habits.

They pelted the buffalo with stones and tried to beat it with sticks, but Kaalan Varky had no idea how to catch and tether it. His anxiety increased when someone mentioned that if the buffaloes ran east for another two kilometres, they would enter the forest and be lost forever. Prabhakaran began reminiscing about the death of Varky's father—who was also known as Kaalan—almost twenty years ago, and Varky listened with a deep sense of shock. It was on the day after one of his buffaloes had escaped into the forest. There was talk that his father's father—Kaalan, as he, too, was known—had also died heartbroken over an escaped animal. What use was Kaalan, the God of Death, if an animal escaped his clutches?

As far back as anyone could remember, Kaalan Varky's ancestors had been butchers. When, over eighty years ago, people from Pala travelled east to clear the forest and claim the land to farm, Varky's grandfather had joined them. In those days, people liked to eat meat but they did not like to associate with the butchers who did the slaughter. At church, they were expected to stand, unobtrusively, in the back row. No one wanted to marry a butcher. Even Varky's dead wife, Eli, had confessed to the priest that their first night together had made her want to vomit.

Varky's grandfather did not join in with the other migrants to clear the forest or to cultivate the land. Instead, he built a roofless enclosure with wooden planks for walls, and slaughtered a buffalo or a pig on alternate fortnights. It was hard to make a living in the early days. When the forest was full of wild boar, wild buffalo and mouse deer, who wanted to eat the meat of domesticated animals! But Varky's grandfather knew no other work, so he persevered. He personally delivered the meat, cut, cleaned and ready for the pot, to his fellow migrants' houses, and accepted whatever they gave as payment—money, rice, root vegetables . . .

Varky's family acquired the nickname 'Kaalan' not because Kaalan, the God of Death, rode on a buffalo, or because they were gods of death to the buffalo. The name was bestowed on them because of a peculiar physical characteristic: their 'kaalu'—legs—that were extraordinarily long, and seemed to sprout right from underneath their armpits. Even today, if he went down the hills into Pala, Varky would have no difficulty recognizing his relatives. From two-year-olds to ninety-year-olds, all of them walked with long steps on their astonishingly long legs. It became customary for neighbours to question the paternity of any long-legged child that was born in the vicinity. Despite the persistent stink of blood, Varky, in his youth, had been quite adept at wooing women, an ability he retained even now as an older man. His liaisons were usually in houses which had four panes to their front doors. Interested women who wanted to invite him in would leave the top two panes unbolted from the inside at around 3 a.m. Varky would open them quietly, swing his long legs over the bottom panes, and enter the house to quickly do the deed and get to the shop in time for the day's slaughter. When the husbands of his paramours came to buy meat, Varky gave them extra pieces of fat and offcuts for free, and the unsuspecting men grew plump on these offerings.

Things became critical when one of the escaped buffaloes kicked over a small fire someone had lit to keep themselves warm. The sparks set fire to a haystack and a barn. The news spread far and wide with the flames and the smoke. Someone said that the bull-buffalo had gored five people and killed one of them. Another story spread that a whole herd of buffaloes had escaped, and they were vengefully attacking humans. Women hugged their children tightly and cowered behind bolted doors while the braver of the men ran out to join the efforts.

After a breakfast of vellayappam and karimeen mappas, Kuriachan was watering the plants and hanging the new, still wet rubber sheets from wire lines to catch the morning sun when he heard the commotion. He did not open the front gate, but pressed his considerable paunch on it and looked into the lane. A large crowd chased after an animal, some bellowing with grave expressions on their faces, and others excited as though they were taking part in a celebration. One of them peeled away from the crowd and prepared to sit down to urinate beneath the curtain of passion flower vines hanging off the boundary wall. Kuriachan beckoned him.

'Who are you? What the hell is going on?'

'Kaalan Varky's buffaloes have gotten loose, a female and a dangerous bull,' the man said as he finished his business. 'Don't open the gate.' He took off after the crowd, leaving Kuriachan in a state of anxiety.

Kuriachan was the first person to start cultivating rubber in the area. Many years ago, when he planted rubber seeds on his land and brought people from the rubber board to help bud the saplings, the elders in the predominantly Christian community who toiled day and night under the steam of dried fish and day-old kanji had found it hilarious.

'Why is he not planting tapioca? Is he going to live on rubber milk instead?' they asked, laughing scornfully at him.

But when, over the following fifteen years, Kuriachan tapped the rubber, bought another couple of pieces of land with the proceeds, expanded his cultivation, and became the owner of a big house and a car, they began to think otherwise. By then, Kuriachan had become more prominent a personage than the heads of households with proud lineages, and although he knew nothing at all about matters other than agriculture, people began to pay heed to his opinions.

Kuriachan's daughter's engagement ceremony was fixed for the next day, a Sunday. She insisted she was not ready to get married, and spent hours talking secretly about higher studies to someone on her mobile phone. But Kuriachan's bullish brain told him that she would change her mind once the engagement was over, even ask him why he had delayed getting her married for this long. Some fifteen guests were expected from the prospective bridegroom's side from Kottayam. Kuriachan had invited only five or six people, including the parish priest, locally. Why give his hillbilly neighbours a chance to display their ignorance in front of the sophisticated Kottayam folk, he had thought. He would make up for it by inviting all and sundry to the wedding and give them a big feast, he told himself. The preparations for the engagement feast were well under way. His wife had already made a curry with motha, a type of kingfish. Two varieties of pickles had been maturing for the last week. The pulisseri would be made in the evening, and the thoran and the challas could be made quickly on the day itself. Kaalan Varky had promised to deliver the best cuts of a freshly slaughtered buffalo to be roasted with turmeric, chilli, coriander and market spices on a slow-burning wood fire, adding ground black pepper and slices of coconut towards the end. Cooked in a bit of pig fat to enhance the flavour until it developed a deep brown hue, the buffalo roast would grace the dining table, making all other curries and accompaniments irrelevant. The news of the runaway buffalo was worrying but he tried to console himself thinking that no four-legged animal had escaped forever from the two-legged one. Checking that the gate was securely bolted, he went back to his work.

It was almost noon, and yet the collective effort to capture the buffaloes had come to nothing. Anthony managed to lasso the bull twice but failed to bring him under control. Varky lost his footing trying to hold on to the rope, cut his forehead open and bruised his knees, and ended up on the veranda of a house where the womenfolk cooled him down with hand fans and gave him water.

Minute by minute, the list of property damaged by the animals became longer. Two autorickshaws, a number of bicycles, three or four hen houses, several vegetable patches, a car shed, countless containers of rubber milk . . . Watching the animals and the crowd running amok through the freshly planted rubber in the church compound, the parish priest rang the bells and made several phone calls to destinations unknown.

Presently, as though ordained by God himself, the land witnessed the complete fall from grace of two of its prominent personages even as one of its lesser citizens emerged from a life of insignificance as though rising from a disused well with the brilliance of the morning sun. The first prominent personage was the leader of the Farmers' Party, a man who presented himself in all crises as a problem-solver. When people went to his house to ask for his help in solving the problem of the buffaloes, he refused to come out and meet them, and sent his wife to the front door to run them off. The second was a retired colonel, a quiet man who caused no harm to anyone. People had long believed, although he had never once made such a claim himself, that he was in possession of a gun. Even burglars left his house alone. In this moment of grave crisis, he, too, let them down, and declared once and for all that retired soldiers were not legally allowed to take their guns home. He promised them a bottle of alcohol from the monthly quota he received from the army as an ex-serviceman, but his fellow countrymen booed in his face.

The man who rose into eminence was an erstwhile small-time rowdy, a man people called 'Peshakan' Shanku—Shanku the Quarrelsome. A few altercations and knife fights had earned him a reputation around thirty years ago. At one point, he began boasting about a murder he had committed. The police picked him up and worked him over, and he had been resting and recuperating ever since. Everyone hated him, especially women, as it was said that he peeped into bathrooms and grabbed their gold ornaments in the cover of darkness. But now, entirely unexpectedly, Peshakan Shanku rose to the occasion, and took over the leadership of the hunt for the escaped animals. Selecting a few of the bravest men, he organized the unruly crowd into two groups, setting one group after each animal, and sent a third group, led by Anthony, in a different direction.

Soon, the groups, under the leadership of Peshakan Shanku and Anthony, closed off all the lanes leading to the forest. Frustrated, one of the animals which had headed east ran back into the junction. Maddened by the shower of stones, he destroyed two paan shops. At the market in the middle of the junction, the crowd had him surrounded. A Tamilian moneylender who arrived once a week to collect the interest from the women in the shops and households he had lent money to, a man known locally as Saturday Man, suddenly found himself in the middle of the melee. He was, by nature, uninterested in anything other than his moneylending business, and had only peeped out to see what was happening, but some conniving person made good use of the occasion and pushed him in front of the enraged buffalo. In the ensuing confusion, the buffalo rammed through the human wall surrounding him and escaped. On the way, he trampled over the martyr's memorial that had been recently erected by the Communist Party, built in the traditional communist style with wooden planks, a red cloth and a pike that pointed sharply towards the sky.

As in all hillside settlements, comrades were few in number but full in strength locally, and it did not take long for them to assemble.

'It's that Kaalan Varky's buffalo,' said the man who looked like their leader.

Ramming his right fist into the air, one of his comrades belted out a slogan.

'Varkicha, you nincompoop,

We'll get you, your time is up . . .'

The others did not take up the slogan.

'There's no need for that,' the leader said. 'It's not his fault that the buffaloes ran off. Poor man, he gave us five hundred rupees for the panchayat elections, remember?'

Besides, Varky never made them wait too long when they went to buy meat.

The sloganeer tried again in a louder voice.

'Buffalocha, you nincompoop

Are you a man, show your face

You'll die without seeing your mother's face . . .'

This time, his comrades took up the slogan, and belting it out at the top of their voices, they set out in a procession towards the police camp. The nearest police station was in a town twenty-five kilometres away, but a battalion of black-clad, gun-bearing policemen had recently set up camp at the government school because of a rumour that a gang, suspected to be armed, had been spotted in the local area. They were not pot-bellied like ordinary policemen, and were often seen marching past the lanes in front of the school or going into the forest in search of the suspected armed men. They spent the rest of the time out of their uniforms, eating, sleeping or playing volleyball.

As soon as he heard the comrades' complaint, the chief of the battalion issued a command in English, and in a matter of seconds several policemen, clad in shiny shoes and impeccable uniforms, stood in attention in front of him.

'See, that's all there's to it,' said the leader to his comrade, the sloganeer. 'Those idiots are running after the buffaloes while these policemen here have machine guns. They'll make quick work of the animals.'

The chief bellowed again, and the policemen divided themselves into two groups and ran to the front and back entrances of the school. They quickly bolted the gates and secured the compound.

'You can leave now,' the chief told the comrades. 'We can't simply shoot the buffaloes. The district collector has to give the order first.'

The policemen returned to their daily duties.

Meanwhile, some others went to the forest office, but there too they were met with disappointment. The forest office could get involved only if the animals were wild, they were told. They were warned, too, that if the animals were killed and they turned out to be wild, everyone involved would be arrested.

All morning, the two buffaloes and the groups of men chasing them had run mostly in two different directions.

But there was one occasion when they all came together. The incident took place in a piece of land, newly hoed and readied to plant tapioca, that belonged to a hard-working farmer who was the father of a young man named Sudheer. Having recently returned home from his studies in Bangalore, Sudheer spent most of his time online. Although he did not know even his next-door neighbours, and his compatriots had hardly set eyes on him in recent years, he had five thousand friends and thousands of followers on Facebook. His father had no use for him, so never asked him to help out with the cultivation.

Clad only in a pair of shorts, Sudheer was on the terraced roof enjoying the mild westering sun when he heard a racket and looked down. In a rising cloud of dust, two buffaloes raced through the compound in which he had never set foot, and a large crowd chased after them. The scene looked like something out of a foreign-language film. Sudheer filmed it on his mobile phone and immediately posted it on Facebook. In a matter of seconds, the post was 'liked' by many people and 'shared' several times all over the world. A girlfriend of his from France commented on the extraordinary things that happened only in India. Lonely, elderly parents marvelled at the phone calls that suddenly began to pour in every half hour from their offspring who were in Australia and Europe working as nurses, asking whether the buffaloes had been captured.

By sundown, there were some positive outcomes, at least for some people, from the havoc wreaked by the buffaloes. The bull-buffalo, ousted by Anthony and his gang from an abandoned coffee plantation, ran down the lane leading away from the white saheb's old estate, and towards Co-operative Bank. The bank was only a small, ugly, shuttered room but it sat inside a compound with a strong boundary wall. Within it were wooden racks stacked with files and ledgers, evidencing the different ways in which local people were in debt of an economic institution. There was also a cupboard that contained money and pawned objects and a couple of computers.

'Let's get the buffalo inside the compound,' Prabhakaran called out. Only the day before, the secretary of the bank had put up a notice for repossession in front of his house and had a couple of people sign it as witnesses.

Pelted with stones from all sides, the buffalo ran into the compound. The sweeper was about to pull the shutter down for the day, and he and the young woman who was the accountant scrambled over the wall and escaped. The animal broke the computers and upturned the furniture. As though to smoke the animal out, some people set fire to brush torches and threw them into the building, and when the wooden racks housing the files and ledgers caught fire, the crowd started shouting in excitement. Watching the unbelievable unfold before their eyes, some of them danced in happiness, and one man among them declared that the heroic buffalo should be left alone and that he was going to contact the politician and animal rights activist Maneka Gandhi.

Just before the day began to darken, the animals disappeared from the sight of the two hunting gangs. It was eerily quiet, not even the flutter of a leaf. Either the animals had collapsed somewhere foaming at the mouths, or they were laying low, hiding in a bush or a hillside. But it was the thought that they had finally entered the forest that worried Anthony. If that was the case, he would not be able to face Varky again. There was no point in searching the forest in the dark. Suddenly, a summer holiday gang of urchins aged twelve years and under ran past the grown-ups wielding small sticks and green twigs.

'Da, what are you doing here? Go home, get!' Anthony shouted.

'The buffalo is in that compound over there,' said one of the children who had fallen behind as he had to hoist up his half pants sliding down his waist as he ran. 'He's hiding.'

Anthony and his gang took off in that direction. The animal must be exhausted, they thought, and decided to bring it down by its legs and kill it on the spot.

'Where is it?' Anthony asked the noisy bunch of children.

'There, look!'

They pointed to the base of a tree. A ten-year-old, dressed only in a pair of knickers, stood on all fours, swinging his tail made of a length of jute string. He was the buffalo, the rest were the hunters. Anthony broke off a twig from a coffee bush, thrashed the children and chased them away.

As darkness descended, the junction and its surroundings turned into festival grounds. Hillsides sparkled with the flickering flames of gas lamps and torches as the search for the animals continued. With the buffaloes as their excuse, young men left their homes, bottles of alcohol in hand, for a quiet evening with their friends. A few young men with extraordinarily shiny faces hung around the houses of their sweethearts in the hope that their fathers and brothers would be out searching for the buffaloes, leaving the young women unattended. Some of them were lucky enough to have their wishes come true. Meanwhile, the ongoing search made some others extremely anxious. It was detrimental to their usual night-time adventures. Wanting to fish in troubled waters, valiant young men from neighbouring villages arrived in jeeps, and ran amok through yards and compounds. The locals who had given up the day's work to join the cause—carpenters, toddy tappers and government employees alike—watched them with trepidation, wondering whether things were getting out of hand. The issue led to a fight between two drunkards at the junction. Several others made use of the occasion to settle months-old scores. But the night was still young, and more eventful and scarier things were yet to happen.

First, there was the death of an old man, a vaidyar who was well known among the older generation for his healing powers and prowess with herbal potions and concoctions. A deeply devout and virtuous man, he had been on his deathbed for over a year. Perhaps it was the disciplined life he had lived, or the prayers of his grateful patients, that even after his body, paralysed on one side, had developed bedsores, his soul refused to leave it.

His children took turns to look after him. In his half-asleep state, he heard one of them say to himself: 'If he had been the type to have a tipple every now and then, he would have gone by now.'

Hearing the uproar of the buffalo hunt, they stepped out to investigate, while he lay alone in his bed on the veranda. In a moment of clear consciousness, he opened his eyes and looked into the yard, and saw a black-hued animal standing there looking straight at him. On the animal's back sat someone splendid, considering him with merciful eyes. Who else could it be on the back of a buffalo other than Kaalan, the God of Death himself? Astoundingly, Vaidyar's emaciated body sat itself up and his palms closed in prayer. 'Bhagavane . . .' he said, and his soul departed for the next world.

Darkness spread, and with it the despair that the confounded people felt. The next day was a Sunday, so it would be evening by the time armed police arrived with the district collector's order. There was no telling what might happen in the meantime, or whether the animals might manage to escape into the deep forest. By then, everyone had started referring to the bull-buffalo as 'he', as though they were not talking about a four-legged domestic animal but about a cunning, vengeful, debauched and exceedingly strong man. Outsiders who had joined the hunt had, by then, taken to throwing lit firecrackers into bushes and compounds and shouting at the top of their voices, and terrified animals ran in all directions wreaking havoc. Men worried about the women and children left alone at home, and women worried about their husbands who might, at any instant, end up in front of a raging buffalo.

Suddenly, someone said the words 'Kuttachan, Kuttachan . . .' It was a name that had been on everyone's mind since the hunt began in the morning, but no one had dared say it aloud. The crowd split into two—one wanting to solicit Kuttachan's help and the other, with

Anthony's voice ringing loudly, dead against it. Kaalan Varky refrained from commenting.

A marksman who never missed his target, Kuttachan was a well-known hunter. There was a time when the area had been known for the top-quality game meat he sold in secret. He also traded in arrack, brewed from palm toddy in stills set up deep in the forest, and a lehyam or jam-like preparation of marijuana. There were many stories about him threatening women who entered the forest searching for a stray goat or to collect firewood with his gun and making them take off their clothes. Eventually, his free reign in the forest came to an end when a forest office was established in the area, and he got embroiled in a dozen cases and had to spend some time in jail. That was when he became Varky's helper at the butchery. The brisk business that went on there surprised him. When he stashed a bundle of ganja in the palm-leaf roof of the shop in an attempt to get rid of Varky by getting him arrested, the local people beat him up and ran him out of the village.

A bunch of people got into a jeep and went over the hills to the other side in search of Kuttachan. The moment he saw them, his eyes glittered in the memories of the local women and the prime agricultural land. Still, he tried to be firm. 'I'll not return there. Not on my life!'

But faced with their entreaties, he soon changed his mind. He picked up his well-oiled, unlicensed double-barrel gun, slung the bag of gunpowder and glass over his shoulder, and set out with them. Two sharp sticks, used to pierce the nose of bulls to put on rings, hung from his waist.

'Why do you need those, Kuttacha?' asked one of the men. 'We're going to kill the buffaloes, aren't we?'

Kuttachan ignored the question.

Like rats behind the pied piper, a brand new set of volunteers followed Kuttachan when he made his appearance dressed in hunting gear—knee-high boots, a pair of trousers with several pockets stuffed with scopes, a rough shirt, and a searchlight attached to his forehead.

'All idiots who have been playing hide-and-seek since morning can go home and sleep,' he said, looking Anthony straight in the face. 'All I need is two bullets. I'll take care of the animals.'

A scuffle ensued, and they began shouting and pushing at each other. As is always the case, most of the people went with the man with the gun. Only four or five people stuck with Anthony, and he smelled danger.

Kaalan Varky had no sons, only a daughter, Sophie. Anthony nursed the secret hope that Sophie, and through her, a considerable fortune, would one day come into his life. This was the only reason Anthony stayed on with Varky, suffering daily abuse. Often, he followed her to the parallel college where she studied. He was beaten up many times for getting into the bus through the front door, which was reserved for women, and travelling without a ticket by pretending to be a policeman. He knew that Varky kept him on only because no one else would forgo their sleep to do all the early-morning chores. He was conscious that Varky never trusted him with any of the important jobs, tasking him only with the chopping of the meat. Anthony felt this night was going to be significant, one that would make or break his life.

But if Kuttachan were to kill the buffaloes . . . Anthony knew that he would then have to go back to a life of day-time sleeping, night-time wandering, and the occasional fishing, while Kuttachan insinuated himself back into the butcher shop and Varky's heart.

As the darkness deepened, the anxiety that had been building up inside Kuriachan turned into full-fledged dread. He realized he could no longer count on Varky to keep his word to deliver the buffalo meat for his daughter's engagement feast first thing in the morning. Even if the animals were to be captured and killed, those who took part in the killing would make away with the meat. Without the roast buffalo meat, Kuriachan would be humiliated in front of his guests from Kottayam. The mere thought of serving them a diminished feast with pulisseri and fish curry made him quake with anger and sorrow. Frustrated, he shouted at his wife for no reason, and gave the cat that was meowing for food a kick for good measure.

When it was almost midnight, Kuriachan stepped out of the house without telling even his wife. He had tied a towel over his head, knotting it under his chin. Four or five compounds away from his house lived Ammini, a woman who had been widowed at a young age, and had, over the years, acquired a bit of a bad reputation. She kept hens, egg layers. It had suddenly occurred to him that he could buy five or six chickens from her, and that, although it would not stand up to the majestic taste of slow-roasted buffalo meat, a chicken piralan would go quite well with the rice.

'Amminiye . . .' Kuriachan knocked on the door.

Ammini opened the door, rubbing her eyes.

'Kuriachan chettan . . . Come on in,' she said, a deep blush spreading across her face.

'It's not . . . that, Ammini. It's . . . chicken . . .'

'It's all right,' she said.

At the exact moment when Ammini took him by his arm to lead him inside, some of those who had followed Kuttachan, armed with sticks and torches, walked down the lane and saw what was happening. Calling Ammini a few choice words, they sent her back inside her house before dealing with Kuriachan. They made him take off his mundu and tie it on his head, and marched him, now dressed only in his underpants, clapping and hooting, to the junction. The task pleased them much more than capturing the escaped animals.

While Kuriachan was on his way to Ammini's house, his daughter, who did not want to get married and had planned her escape, was making a phone call to her friend. Her friend, an adventurous young man from Thodupuzha, came to pick her up on his motorbike. They had only moved a hundred yards when the cow-buffalo rushed at them and tossed over the motorbike. Arriving at the scene precisely at that moment, the morality enforcers set upon the young man, enraged at the audacity of the outsider. Chased back home, Kuriachan entered the house by the back door while his daughter returned by the front door.

After a long search, Kuttachan came upon the bull-buffalo by a rocky outcrop, but he missed his first shot. Blaming it on the man helping him load the gun, he got ready for a second shot. As though single-handedly facing up to a large army, he silenced the crowd with a long whistle.

Crouching down behind a rock, he took careful aim. This time, the shot hit the end of the buffalo's tail and the animal took off, with a loud snort, down the hill. Destroying the lean-tos behind two houses and the windshield of a car on his way, he disappeared into the darkness. Loud screams emanated from the houses along the way.

Realizing that the number of people following his lead was depleting by the minute, Anthony, meanwhile, tried to cook up new plans. For many years, his routine was to sleep during the day and spend the nights wandering around, so he knew the sounds and stirrings of the dark intimately. Night prowlers had no use for roads, so it was through the compounds of houses that he routinely moved. He had come across many sights, faces, people and creatures in his journeys, but he paid them scant attention. He knew the lay of the land in the dark better than anyone else. Putting this knowledge to good use, Anthony and his men combed through compounds, bushes, deserted firewood stores, cattle barns, and even the outdoor toilets. His companions watched with amazement as he moved swiftly and confidently across terraced agricultural compounds, fences and slippery embankments riddled with foot-trapping holes. Finally, when he came across one of the animals, he had his men surround it, silently and keeping to the shadows. They persuaded it, skilfully and quietly, into the compound nearby. Anthony was familiar with the disused well in the overgrown south-eastern corner of that compound. Herded into that corner by the men surrounding it, the buffalo fell into the well with a terrible roar.

'Anthony has caught the buffalo!'

Unable to contain his excitement, one of the men shouted. In the darkness, his voice reverberated across the hillsides. It brought others trampling through the compound, and in a matter of minutes, the bushes around the well were cut down.

'It's normal that buffaloes fall into wells,' Kuttachan remarked, shining his torch into the overgrown interior of the well. He pointed his gun into it. 'Let's kill it and then pull it up.'

'That won't be necessary,' Anthony said, pissed off that his accomplishment in trapping the buffalo was not being met with sufficient appreciation. 'If I can trap it in the well, I know how to bring it up also. Alive!'

Kuttachan noticed that the majority of the crowd agreed with Anthony, so he stood aside as though ready to watch the performance unfold. Some people went about organizing a pulley and strong ropes to use as nooses, while others began pelting the trapped animal with stones. A couple of people dragged big rocks over and chucked them into the well, enjoying the sound of them falling on the body of a living creature. Others threw in lit brush torches.

Eventually, two men armed with nooses and headlights were lowered carefully into the well, guided by the ropes tied around their waists and passed through the pulley. Advice poured in from the onlookers. Don't step on the ground . . . Beware of snakes . . . They toiled in the darkness of the well for almost an hour before being pulled back up.

'It's the cow-buffalo,' one of them said. There was a tinge of disappointment behind the satisfaction in his voice.

After a long time and a lot of effort, the men pulled the buffalo up, her forelegs, middle of the body and hindquarters noosed, on to planks laid over the mouth of the well and on to solid ground. Her body was covered in bruises, and blood leaked from her head where the horn had broken off. As soon as Anthony tied a rope around her neck and removed the nooses from her body, people set upon her, beating her with whatever sticks they could find, and cruelly poking the animal in her private parts.

At that precise moment, an astonishing thing took place, something that the assembled crowd would remember till the end of their days, and which would become part of the local folklore. At first, they thought that a storm was rushing towards them from the darkness of the coffee plantation, but before they could wonder whether they should take shelter or get drenched, something dark and frighteningly loud charged through the crowd. Some lost their footing and fell into the well, while others were tossed away. The gaslights and torches that had lit up the compound went up into the air before falling on the ground and extinguishing. Anthony was thrown into the thorny tangle of a thudali bush, and by the time he regained his footing and his composure, the bull-buffalo and his rescued companion were three compounds away. Torch in hand, Kuttachan was seen running after them, cursing at the top of his voice.

Before the tarmacked road ended, a footpath veered off it steeply down through a rubber plantation. Where it reached a creek, and before the next climb, there was a waterhole by a cluster of rocks and a bamboo thicket.

Kuttachan was convinced that the buffaloes were at that spot.

'Don't you all come rushing down,' he said as he walked down the slope, gun held firmly in his left hand. 'You want to come?' he asked Raman, an old footballer, holding out the bag he had slung over his shoulder. 'Just hang on to this.'

At the end of the footpath, they walked silently to the cluster of rocks with their torches switched off. The bamboo thicket rustled as though there was an elephant in it. Crouching, they stepped carefully towards it.

Distracted by a strange noise, Raman looked behind him, and when he turned back, he felt that Kuttachan, who had been to his left, was not there any more. He put his hand out and searched in the dark. Nothing! Perplexed, he stood there unsure whether to move forward or go back. Suddenly, eyes glowed in the darkness in front of him. Before he could figure out if it was man or buffalo, before he recalled that it was him who had told the police about Kuttachan all those years ago, Kuttachan plunged the two sharp sticks he had brought with him when he came to the hunt into either side of Raman's stomach.

As the others heard the screams and started running down the footpath, Kuttachan came up towards them carrying Raman over his shoulder.

'The buffalo got him,' he said, laying Raman on the road.

'Buffalo can't gore from both sides like this,' Anthony said.

No one paid him any attention. 'Are you here to catch them or to protect them?' someone asked. The cow-buffalo's escape had made them suspicious of his intentions.

The calamity at the well and Raman's stabbing had taken place in the second half of the night, and yet the news reached far and wide in a matter of minutes. It sent the entire community into a mad panic. Expecting an attack at any moment, the elderly in the houses sat wide awake behind locked doors. Some set bonfires in their yards to keep the animals away, while others banged on tin cans and created an almighty ruckus. The police station and the fire station were inundated with phone calls. Even those who usually stayed well clear of everything except what affected them directly began running around all over the place, armed with lengths of firewood, machetes, hatchets, crowbars and objects with dubious usefulness under the circumstances such as cluster-hooks used to retrieve things from wells, chopping knives, pickaxes, iron pots, ropes, hoes, sickles and shovels. It was not clear from their actions whether their intention was to capture the animals or to drive them away because even as they wielded weapons, they created a racket screaming and shouting, and banging on things. Raman's brothers announced that, when caught, the animals should be released to them so that they could torture them to death. One of them tried to beat up Anthony. The whole land was awake and excited as never before, not even for the annual festival at the church. Houses were drenched in light and songs and celebratory shouts rang out.

Finally, just before dawn, it began to seem that their combined efforts were coming to fruition. The two buffaloes ran up from two directions into an open meadow. To the east of it was the forest, and in between the meadow and the forest was a deep cleft strewn with rocks at the bottom. The men had them trapped within a human wall that closed off the other three sides. Soon, tired from the relentless shower of stones, the animals came to a halt and, like criminals in front of a firing squad, stood still, facing the rock-strewn cleft. A cloud of flies buzzed over the wound where the cow-buffalo's horn had broken off. She looked exhausted, and when she folded her front knees in an attempt to sit down, someone chucked a knife at her and made her get up. The bull swished the remnant of his tail in an attempt to ward of the flies. Strings of foam hung down from the corner of his mouth, and he opened and closed his eyes as though he was going to graze through the entire meadow.

Kuttachan was ready with his gun. He had no doubt that, this time, his bullets would find their target. He commanded the crowd to take two steps back. Two men stood ready with sledgehammers. As soon as the animals were shot down, they were to crack their skulls so that they would not rise again.

Suddenly, Bhanu the bull-buffalo turned around and faced the crowd. They felt that there was a new expression of determination on his face. The gun trembled in Kuttachan's hand. Before he could make a decision, producing a cry that was unnatural for buffaloes and with what seemed like supernatural strength, Bhanu rushed forward. More than half of the crowd of enthusiasts turned tail and ran away. Peshakan

Shanku, who had been at the forefront of the efforts thus far, was the first to take off. The human wall that had extended to all three sides dispersed and gathered together in one place. The cow-buffalo seemed confused at first, but then she ran through the gap to the south, turned east, and disappeared into the forest. No one actually saw her flight.

For the next few minutes, a full-frontal fight ensued between the humans and buffalo. Shaking off their panic, people regrouped and confronted Bhanu with weapons. He lowered his head and rammed into them, tossed several men aside, kicked with all four of his legs, gored them left and right, and trampled over the fallen bodies. As he jumped up in the air, even the most brave-hearted among them cried out in amazement. Trying to catch his legs in a noose, Anthony was kicked to the ground. Kuttachan lost his gun in the melee, but he faced off valiantly with the buffalo. Like a seasoned jallikkattu fighter, he grabbed the buffalo by his horns, and tried to bend his neck and bring him kneeling to the ground. Others pitched in to help, and for a while it seemed as though the buffalo was finally defeated. But, digging in his forelegs, the buffalo shook them off, scooped Kuttachan up with his horns and tossed him away. People would say later that, as Kuttachan fell, his intestines were visible through the wound where the horns had torn into him. They tied him up to a bamboo stretcher and took him away to the hospital.

With Kuttachan's departure, the crowd began to lose steam. Anthony made other plans. He stationed men with weapons to the south and west and closed off the exits. Then he came back to the fight.

'Stop!' he shouted at the crowd as though a harmless snake had suddenly found its hood. 'Haven't you had enough? Let him be! Let him go off into the forest.'

Calling out obscenities at Anthony, most of the crowd began to walk away. Dodging the others, the buffalo ran northwards through the gap Anthony had created. The greenery of the forest, almost within grasp, reflected in his tired eyes.

The gap Anthony had created led to a creek that emptied into a swamp. The buffalo swam across the water and began walking into the sticky mud. Soon, his pace slowed, and he made a failed attempt to push down with his forelegs to raise the hind legs. By then, walking with slow, high steps, Anthony was upon him. With the crowd baying all around them, the scene looked like the arena in an ancient empire where an enslaved gladiator faced off a fearsome creature in a deadly fight. Indifferent to the fact that he had no underclothes on, Anthony took off his lungi and tied it around the buffalo's face. Someone threw him a large knife, and he rammed it into the buffalo's chest, piercing through the creature's heart and lung.

As some of the spectators hoisted Anthony up in the air and danced in celebration, others tied ropes to the carcass and dragged it out of the mud. By the time the day broke and the sun was warm, people were seen going back to their houses carrying large chunks of buffalo meat, with the glow of victory on their faces.

The cow-buffalo that had escaped into the inner forest stumbled into the sight of a four-or-five-member gang. Frustrated by mosquito bites, blood-sucking leeches and hunger, they were squabbling with one another.

'See what happened?' asked one of the men. 'We can't get out now. The police are everywhere, and we'll be arrested for entering the forest illegally. You said the whole community will support us. So now, where are they?'

'Look, there it is,' said another, catching sight of the buffalo. 'Catch it!'

The buffalo gathered up her strength and took off, and the hungry men chased after her.

The next Sunday, Kaalan Varky's butcher shop was busy as usual, but there were some small but significant changes. Anthony had become Kaalan Anthony. He did not bother getting married to Sophie. They just started living together in her room. Anthony prepared the meat and chucked large chunks of it at Varky who, with an expression of respect, chopped them up for the customers.

'Buffaloes . . . They've always been dangerous creatures,' Prabhakaran joked as he stood around waiting for his meat. 'A long time ago, it was buffaloes that scuppered a plan of ours to attack a police station. Some of us had armed ourselves and surrounded the station in the night. Suddenly, we heard the sound of an approaching battalion of soldiers marching down the street, and we took off immediately. Turned out, it was a bunch of buffaloes meant for the night market being herded down the street!'

Calling out an appropriate obscenity, Anthony gave him an additional piece of liver.

night watch

Sankunniyaasan was having his supper—a bowl of kanji made with broken rice with a bit of coconut milk mixed in—when he heard about Madhavan's death. A grain of rice got stuck in his throat, aggrieved already by long years of beedi smoking, and he dislodged it by coughing loudly. He had another pinch of mango chammanthi and chased it down with a spoonful of kanji before getting up slowly and walking to the water pipe outside to wash his hands. All the while, his wife stared at him, carefully watching the expression on his face. As he stood wiping his hands on the edge of his mundu, Sankunniyaasan was overcome with a desire to be at the house of the dead man before anyone else could get there. His heart beat faster as this thought took hold, and he grabbed his shirt, ensured there was money in its pocket, and walked hurriedly into the darkness. Watching him leave without a torch to light his way, his wife felt the mild sense of concern that close relatives of elderly people are known to experience.

The dead man's house was just a couple of hundred metres away. Sankunniyaasan walked down the lane at the boundary between the two properties and climbed up to the main road. It was only after 8 p.m., but perhaps because it was a holiday, the road, well-lit with street lights, was deserted except for a pack of dogs in heat, nipping and quibbling and flirting with each other. 'Piss off, dog!' Sankunniyaasan shooed them away, and two or three fearless ones in the pack came towards him, growling menacingly. Usually they were so nervous that they ran away as soon as one pretended to pick up a stone. Turning frequently to watch whether they were following him, Sankunniyaasan walked away quickly. The obvious fear of the most intelligent species of animal when isolated pleased the dogs, and they barked at him in unison.

Only a couple of neighbours had arrived at the house of the deceased before him. A close acquaintance of Sankunniyaasan was in a corner of the front yard, busily making phone calls. Another person stood around, his arms folded and his face suffused with a calamitous expression. The soft sobs of the wife and daughter-in-law of the deceased emanated from the house. A child, the grandson, sat on the bare earth in the front yard, celebrating the rare opportunity to be out in the open at night by digging small holes in the dust.

Sankunniyaasan stepped inside the house. The women stopped crying and looked at each other. They were completely unprepared for his presence. Except for his partially open eyes, Madhavan did not look dead. His big toes were not tied together, nor was there a piece of cloth tied from under his chin to the top of his head. His hands were not folded over his navel in the required humble, supplicating manner. Sankunniyaasan stepped promptly out of the room, tapped on the shoulder of the man talking on the phone and brought him back inside. The man, an office-bearer of the community association, snatched a mundu hanging on the clothes line, tore strips out of it, and made the required knots on the dead body.

'Go get a white mundu,' Sankunniyaasan said, turning to the women.

One of them let out a sob and went to open an almirah in another room.

By then, several people had arrived, and they stood around in the room, on the veranda and in the yard, talking, as tradition demanded, in soft voices or saying nothing at all. The deceased man's son, who had gone into town to buy something, returned, and abandoning his scooter in the front yard, rushed into the room. He looked at his father's dead body, and turned and looked, with a shocked expression, at Sankunniyaasan. It was clear that the presence of the old man shocked him more than the death of his father, unexpected although he was of advanced age.

'Vijayan, fetch a white mundu, quickly,' Sankunniyaasan told the younger man as though they talked to each other every day.

Vijayan was middle-aged, respectable and worldly with an extraordinary sense of humour and patience even amidst the trials of life. He stroked his beard and looked at the deceased for some more time before going in search of the mundu.

When it was brought to him, Sankunniyaasan held it up against the light and examined it. Unfolding it fully, he stood by the side of the bed, and like an experienced fisherman casting his net, he threw it over the body, covering it from neck to feet. As he adjusted the cloth, he looked into Madhavan's half-closed eyes and curled his lips in a derisive smile. 'I've finally defeated you,' he said in his mind, and his skin broke out in goosebumps. At that time, those around him were not thinking about the deceased but about what might be going through Sankunniyaasan's mind.

No one knew exactly when Sankunniyaasan and Madhavan became enemies. There was no point in asking the two people involved. Very few of their contemporaries were left who knew enough about their lives, and their memories were not all that clear. It was also unclear what had caused their enmity in the first place. Enmities usually happen when those who are involved in the same profession or have similar interests encroach upon each other's advancement. But these two men had entirely different lives and circumstances. Madhavan's wife remembered that, around sixty years ago, when their marriage was being fixed, a relative had commented that the bridegroom was a good man except for a long-standing dispute with someone that led to court cases and altercations.

This sentiment was known to be true of Sankunniyaasan as well. On the fourth day after his own wedding, he and his wife had set out on the customary visit to his wife's house. In those days, to reach Harippad where his wife's folk lived, one had to go by boat, first from Kottayam to Alappuzha, and then to Thakazhi. As he stepped out of the boat in Alappuzha, Sankunniyaasan lost his footing and fell, scraping the skin on his forehead and knees like a child at play. He scrambled up, chucked the towel on his shoulder into the canal, and took himself to Thirumala Devaswam Hospital.

'What happened?' the doctor asked him, wiping his wounds with a ball of cotton dipped in a colourful medicine. 'Did you have a tumble?'

'No,' Sankunniyaasan replied. 'I was set upon and beaten.'

He then went to the police station. 'I don't understand why Madhavan would come all the way to Alappuzha to attack you,' the inspector remarked disbelievingly.

'The Ambalapuzha temple festival is going on, no? He must have come for that,' Sankunniyaasan replied without even an inkling of embarrassment. 'He didn't just attack me. He also stole my towel, a madhurakkavini neryathu that I had over my shoulder. Ask her, she saw him do it,' he said, pointing to his wife.

That night, his wife asked him angrily: 'Why did you make up such a thing?'

'Last week, he got an injunction barring me from using the road to our own house. Now let him suffer going in and out of courts for the next five or six years.'

As Sankunniyaasan stepped out of the room where the deceased lay, the assembled mourners felt that a rare energy was emanating from his body. Normally, he was not the type of person who looked to attract attention in such situations. But now, catching sight of the local newspaper agent Raju, his face shone brighter.

'Vijayan,' he looked into the room through the window and called softly. 'Find a photograph of your father. Hurry up. If you give it now, they'll put it in the newspaper tomorrow.'

He led Raju to a table and helped him compose an obituary, consulting Vijayan on the details of Madhavan's children and their spouses. Then, making sure that no one stood close enough to overhear him, he touched Raju's arm.

'He was an absolute scoundrel, you know,' he said as though revealing a secret. 'The trouble he caused me . . .'

'Well, that's not something I can put in the newspaper,' Raju said, laughing.

A law clerk, a comparatively younger man among the mourners who had arrived, came up to Raju when Sankunniyaasan moved away. 'Their case is in the syllabus for the students at the law college,' he said. 'They are a rare breed these days.'

He told Raju that some people found court cases and the law itself as addictive as alcohol and women. Sankunniyaasan had been so involved in legal matters that he was felicitated at the ninetieth birthday celebrations of an important lawyer.

Presently, funeral preparations began as the deceased had no close relatives to arrive from far away except for a sister who lived abroad. But she was unable to come as she had only gone back a month or so ago. Woodcutters arrived and walked around the compound looking for a suitable tree to cut down for the funeral pyre. Sankunniyaasan led the way, torch in hand, with great enthusiasm.

'We'll need plenty of firewood,' he said, aiming his torch at the canopy of a large mango tree. 'His heart was hard as stone. Won't burn easily.'

'In that case, better make sure there's a big enough tree in your own yard,' one of the woodcutters retorted, making everyone laugh.

The woodcutter pushed at the tree with his hand as though checking its strength. They began discussing, as they were wont to do in the houses of the newly deceased, the differences in funeral rites in various lands.

'Mango wood is best,' one opined. 'It has a sap that burns quickly.'

If that was the case, why not use rubber wood, someone said, annoying the whole group. Another person informed them that kings were cremated in pyres of sandalwood, and swamis and bishops were buried in a seated position.

The person who was to lead the rites and rituals the next day was an old-timer, a reactionary who refused to use a mobile phone. A young man, with hair that was combed to a sharp point gazing at the sky and pants that hung way below his waist, started his motorbike to fetch him. Without asking for permission, Sankunniyaasan plonked himself behind him on the motorbike. Having experienced a traumatizing glimpse of the extent of the enmity between Madhavan and Sankunniyaasan only a week before, the young man tried his best to get him off, but to no avail.

The incident had taken place in front of the paan shop in a building with a tiled roof and a row of rooms at the small junction. As people living in the same community, there were occasions when Sankunniyaasan and Madhavan could not avoid being in each other's presence or engaging in conversations with their mutual acquaintances. When such situations arose, each one behaved as though the other was not present, carefully avoiding eye contact, while the other people present avoided, equally carefully, subjects that were of interest to either of them and only talked about general issues.

The lean-to behind the paan shop was where a group of older people played cards. The owner of the paan shop, who was unlucky enough to have lost his leg in a vehicle accident, was the organizer of the games, which were essentially just a way to pass time, where the wagers were so small as to not hurt anyone's pockets. The players sat in a circle on gunny sacks and newspapers spread on the broken and pitted floor. The lean-to was empty except for a couple of sacks of fertilizers meant for the paddy fields nearby, and an old aluminium barrel with a tap left behind from the arrack trade. Madhavan was a regular at these games while Sankunniyaasan took part once or twice a month. On the occasions when both were present, they sat frowning at their cards without joining in the jokes or laughter. If the group took out a collection for a round of drinks, one of them would quietly withdraw and walk away. This state of affairs went on for years, and in all that time, no one had seen them talk to each other or quarrel publicly.

One day, when the game ended and the players began to disperse, it so happened that the two of them were the last to leave. Suddenly, there was a loud noise, and when those who had already stepped out of the lean-to turned back, they saw a fascinating sight. The two old men stood facing each other like gamecocks ready for the attack. It was clear that one of them had broken the unspoken rule of complete silence between them. Others watched as the calamity, always anticipated but never truly expected to materialize, unfolded. It was the end of the day, and a few women on their way back from work and a handful of young people who had come to buy paan were also among the audience. What ensued was a war of words that lasted at least an hour and a half.

The people assembled there, between them, would have had eight or ten swear words in their vocabulary. Perhaps three or four of these words would truly enrage people, the others being mildly objectionable ones bandied about jovially between friends. The performance that the old men put up was beyond anything they could have collectively imagined. They began with a few choice but ordinary words, but the sparks from these spread until a forest fire of larger and meatier words blazed as the enemies turned into wizards who conjured up new and imaginative obscenities, slicing and splicing existing ones. Assaulted by constructions beyond their wildest imagination, the women in the vicinity ran away. Young men enjoyed the performance for a while, but soon they too scrambled on to their motorbikes and fled, unable to withstand the intensity of the battering and scared that the filth pouring out would affect even their manhood.

The smut was all-encompassing. New words with mind-boggling meanings took birth, involving fathers, mothers, sisters, wives, sons, daughters, brothers-in-law, uncles, aunties, ancestors, animals, birds, fish, trees, arthropods such as the cockroach and the centipede, ants, snakes, food items, domestic appliances, diseases, places, days of the week, years, ocean, sky, earth, stars, the sun and the moon, the rain and the wind. Even ordinary words transformed into skin-curling abuse. They did not spare ghosts, saints, gods, priests, caste names, film stars or politicians. Not even universally respected personages such as Gandhi and Nehru were left out. Roiled by revulsion, a young woman, on her way back from college, vomited. Those who were still listening to the barrage of blight felt that all the words they had spoken, or would ever speak, in their entire lives were forever filthy.

In the end, gesturing dramatically with his hands, Sankunniyaasan uttered a phrase that annihilated all moral values in the collective mind of the audience. It pushed them to thoughts of suicide. There was, they felt, nothing more that could be said.

Madhavan ran into the shop, grabbed the knife used to chop tobacco, and came back out. Murder, they thought, the only possible response to Sankunniyaasan's final utterance. But Madhavan walked into the yard behind the shop, and came back with the tapered half of a njalipoovan banana leaf. He placed it ceremoniously in front of Sankunniyaasan, and as though serving a feast for a special occasion, he delivered a response that could not have been possible even in the farthest reaches of a nightmare. The paan shop owner pulled down the shutters of the shop, and the remaining onlookers dispersed. It was a simple phrase, yet one so intricate that it defied interpretation, and so imaginative that it would have put epic poets to shame. The more one thought about it, the more it insinuated itself in one's mind and ate away, like a tapeworm, at one's essence until only death could come to the rescue. Rendered, finally, speechless, Sankunniyaasan walked away hanging his head in shame.

As the night wore on, people began to leave the deceased's house. Some left because there was nothing they could do. Others felt obliged to stay on, and then stepped outside as though to take care of something urgent, and promptly went home and slept. Madhavan's son Vijayan walked into the yard and looked around for Sankunniyaasan. His presence was as uncomfortable to Vijayan as it had been to the deceased. But there he was, sitting under the tarpaulin awning, sipping the black coffee brought over by a neighbour and chatting with some others.

'Have some,' he said to the person sitting next to him. 'Will keep you awake.'

It was late when Sankunniyaasan's son arrived. After viewing the body and paying his respects, he said something to the dead man's son, and walked up to Sankunniyaasan. Together, they moved to a corner of the awning, away from prying ears.

'What are you doing here?' he asked his father. There was alcohol on his breath. 'Go home, why don't you?'

'Well, how can I? If I didn't come, people would blame me. And now that I am here, that too is to blame?' Sankunniyaasan was angry.

His son grabbed his arm and twisted it. 'You old scoundrel! Everyone knows what you're up to,' he said and stomped off in a huff.

Things quietened again after the few latecomers left. Sankunniyaasan was alone in the yard. Occasional sobs and sighs could be heard from the room where the dead body was laid out. A heavy rain fell in the thick darkness and water flowed into the yard. Sankunniyaasan looked at where the yard joined the compound, and thought if he stoked up the mud there, he could stop the water from entering the yard. No one was around, so he searched for a spade in the dark corners behind the house. The dampness closed up his throat, and he stood leaning on a pillar and lit a beedi. The veranda, used to store useless items, appeared and disappeared in the meagre light of his beedi as he sucked at it until, as he took a last puff, it was put out by a droplet of rain that fell with precision on its glowing end.

A sound attracted his attention and he walked to the back of the house. In the sheet-roofed part of the backyard, four or five young men sat drinking alcohol. He stood there for a while like a shadow separated from its body, but they paid him no attention. He could not make out what they were saying or laughing about. Only as he turned away did one of them call out, 'Want a drink, Grandad?'

Back under the awning, he sat watching the rain die down. Soon, the backyard too was plunged into silence, leaving only the faint breeze and the buzz of night-time critters. He dozed off, only for a moment, but when he opened his eyes, he felt as though he had been asleep for a very long time. He scrambled up anxiously and walked to the room where the dead body was laid out. The dead man's wife was asleep on the floor beside the bed. She seemed to be sobbing in her sleep. There was no one else around.

Sankunniyaasan could not remember the last time he was alone with Madhavan. He stared at the dead man's face. Was that really his face? He looked like a complete stranger.

Sankunniyaasan did not participate in the funeral rites the next day. He went into town, very early in the morning, to meet with some people. Later, he presented himself at the police station with copies of various legal documents and made a declaration. He returned home and had lunch, and then went to a piece of land a little distance from his house. His last legal altercation with Madhavan was about another piece of land adjacent to this property. He had tried to solicit the help of a couple of labourers but everyone had refused. So, for the next few hours, he toiled alone, taking apart the fence between the properties and moving it farther away to appropriate the disputed piece of land. By then, Vijayan returned home from the funeral, and someone told him what Sankunniyaasan had done.

'Never mind,' he said. 'His son and I can solve the matter over a bottle of something.'

Sankunniyaasan spent the next day at home, anxiously awaiting some kind of response to his actions. By evening, he was taken to the hospital with a high fever and breathing trouble.

'What's happening?' Raju, the newspaper agent, asked one of his relatives. 'Will we have a news item saying "Arch-enemies die within days of each other"?'